FINDING MY PLACE
One Girl's Strength at Vicksburg

Margo L. Dill

To Ava Westfall— May you always find your place in life! Happy reading— your mom helped me write this book! ☺

Margo Dill 10-21-12

WHITE MANE KIDS
SHIPPENSBURG, PENNSYLVANIA

The acid-free paper used in this book meets the guidelines for permanence and durability of the Committee on Production Guidelines for Book Longevity of the Council on Library Resources.

For a complete list of available publications
please write
White Mane Kids
Division of White Mane Publishing Company, Inc.
P.O. Box 708
Shippensburg, PA 17257-0708 USA
or visit our online catalog www.whitemane.com

Library of Congress Cataloging-in-Publication Data

Dill, Margo L., 1971-
  Finding my place : one girl's strength at Vicksburg / Margo L. Dill.
    p. cm.
  Includes bibliographical references and discussion questions.
  ISBN 978-1-57249-408-4 (softcover : acid-free paper)
  1.Vicksburg (Miss.)--History--Siege, 1863--Juvenile fiction.
[1. Vicksburg (Miss.)--History--Siege, 1863--Fiction. 2. Family life--Mississippi--Fiction. 3. Brothers and sisters--Fiction. 4. Mississippi--History--Civil War, 1861-1865--Fiction.] I. Title.
  PZ7.D5772Fin 2012
  [Fic]--dc23
                                                    2011053430

PRINTED IN THE UNITED STATES OF AMERICA

To Thursday Writers and Columbia Novels Group—
Thank you for your advice, critique, and support.

To My Family—
I dedicate this to you with love.

— Contents —

— PART 1 —
War in Vicksburg, Mississippi

— CHAPTER 1 —
Under Attack

"To the cave, children!" Ma shouted.

Yankees' shells fell from the sky one after another. I dropped my spoon into the cornmeal batter as a tin of flour crashed to the floor. James and Sara jumped up from their game of dominoes and tipped the table.

"To the cave?" I yelled.

"Anna, just go," Ma said as another tin fell off the shelf—this time spilling sugar on the stove.

She opened the door, and we sprinted across the backyard as fast as jackrabbits running from a hunter. Ma led the way, and I went last, pushing Sara along. Her short, six-year-old legs didn't move fast enough, so I scooped her up. Ma and James covered their heads with their arms as if that would protect them from a shell.

When we reached the cave, we ran inside and huddled together. Everyone breathed heavy but stayed real quiet. I wondered where our servants, George and his son, Noah, were and then remembered Ma had sent them on an errand earlier. I hoped they were somewhere safe. Some people didn't care whether their slaves lived or died; I was glad we didn't treat George and Noah that way. They had come to work for us after our grandfather died.

They built this cave for us after General Grant bombed the city a few months before. Rumors flew around town that he wasn't going to give up until he took Vicksburg. So, George and Noah dug a large room out of a yellow clay hill behind our house, like most other slaves did for their families. Then, they added boards across the top for support and more on the bottom for a floor. We could all stand upright inside, except George.

Ma told them to place a few chairs, a small table, and our favorite rocker inside. Jars of water rested on a small shelf along with some candles. We ran a rope from one side to the other and hung a sheet on it, separating the room into two parts. Three small spring mattresses and a trunk full of candles, a quilt, and a tiny mirror lay on the floor on one side.

It didn't seem to matter what we put in there; the cave was still a gloomy hole instead of a home. Our things felt damp, and it smelled like rain. George and Noah had even made two openings to let more air through and to have another exit in case of a cave-in, but it was still dark and stuffy.

Ma inspected the work when they had finished since Pa and my older brother, Michael, were gone fighting with the army. "I feel closed in," she told us. "We won't ever go there unless we're in terrible danger."

We must be in terrible danger, then, since we had run to this cave today. I didn't want any of us to have to stay here or eat here or sleep here tonight. It was a horrible way to spend a day. I hated the Yankees.

James stood at the entrance and looked up in the sky. "Those stupid Yankees messed up my dominoes game, and I was beating Sara, too."

He always thought of himself, like his dumb game was more important than the Blue Bellies trying to take over. There was such a big difference between me and James, even though he was eleven—only two years younger than me.

"James, hush up," I said. "If Grant takes over our city, he won't let boats bring supplies to us. We'll be in big trouble then, and you'll be complaining about how hungry you are."

"Ma, I'm scared." Sara took Ma's hand.

"Anna, that's enough," Ma said. "Away from the exit, James. There's nothing to worry about in here. Our soldiers will take care of this in a few—"

Shots from the cannons cut off Ma's words. I flinched and huddled closer to her. James and Sara did the same. Tears fell from my sister's eyes as she grabbed onto Ma's skirt.

Ma started singing "Bonnie Blue Flag."

> *"Hurrah! Hurrah!*
> *For Southern rights hurrah! Hurrah!*
> *For the Bonnie Blue flag that bears a single star.*
> *Hurrah! Hurrah!"*

"*Hurrah! Hurrah!*" We joined in.

We held hands and danced around the cave, singing louder and louder to drown out the blasts from the cannons. Sweat clung to Ma's lip, but for once, she didn't seem to mind her unladylike appearance.

"Maybe Pa and Michael will come here and fight," James said when we stopped singing. "I miss them." Tears poured out of Sara's eyes, and I wondered if she would ever have enough to fill up her sadness.

"I miss them, too." But I swallowed the lump in my throat because I knew they had done the right thing by joining the army last year. We needed to protect our land from the Yanks. Pa and Michael couldn't stand by and let other men do the fighting.

"That's enough," Ma said again. She hated talking about them, like if she didn't think about it, she wouldn't miss them or worry about them coming back.

Shells still crackled through the air as if we were in the middle of a terrible thunderstorm. "You might as well get comfortable," Ma said. "We're not going anywhere for a while."

We all sat down on one of the mattresses. James kicked my foot, but I ignored him. As I listened to the noise outside, I knew we were in trouble. It didn't sound like Grant would give up anytime soon. He would keep shooting at us until he got what he wanted.

— Chapter 2 —
The Soldiers' Retreat

Two weeks later

"Mama!" Sara screamed as she ran in the front door.

My stomach knotted with worry, and I remembered Sara crying almost as hard a few weeks ago when we had to escape to our cave. We had to stay there for hours and hours, and I felt sicker and sicker the longer we were there. My stomach had turned over every time I heard a shell flying, and my mouth felt like I hadn't had a drink of water in days. I didn't want to go to that underground hole ever again.

"Mama!" Sara burst into the kitchen with tears streaming down her cheeks. A strand of blonde hair, like mine, hung in her face as she tugged on Ma's skirt and pulled her toward the door. With her other hand, my sister clutched her rag doll, Betty.

Why was she carrying on like this? Sure, she cried all the time. But the only other time she had acted this way was when James fell from the oak tree, busting his nose and an arm. Blood had covered his face, and she thought he was dying.

"Mama, come on," she said.

While Ma and I had been fixing supper, I heard the army troops on the road outside our house. But that was nothing unusual. Soldiers had been marching in and out of Vicksburg for the past six months.

Sara must have seen something awful. I prayed it wasn't Pa or Michael hurt . . . or worse. Yesterday, one of my schoolmates heard that her eighteen-year-old brother wasn't ever coming home again. He was killed in a battle with the North somewhere, and he was the same age as Michael. There was nothing left of his body to send home to be buried.

I couldn't imagine that happening to my brother. "God, please don't let them be outside, wounded or even . . . please. Let them be safe."

"Whatever's the matter with you?" Ma asked as Sara pulled her along. James followed them closely through the dining room and parlor.

I didn't follow. I'd find out soon enough what was so terrible, and right now, I'd rather not know. I checked on the biscuits in the oven, even though I usually didn't care much for cooking.

I'd had to help out a lot more since our house servant, Nellie, died. She went to Heaven about a month ago, trying to have a baby that went, too. George had come running to the house, asking Ma to help. My siblings and I had to stay inside, but we watched the servants' quarters through the kitchen window.

After just a few minutes, Noah, who was the same age as James, came out and sat real still on a log stump in the backyard. Then he lowered his head, and his whole body shook—his sobs came right through our open window like a thousand hornets stinging me everywhere. George came out and picked up his son, who already stood as tall as his pa's shoulders. We loved Nellie so much. I missed her cooking and funny stories. Since then, I helped Ma prepare meals but wasn't half as good as Nellie. James told me so every time we sat down to the table.

Once I made sure the biscuits were fine, I started cleaning up our mess in the kitchen. I was not going outside to see Pa or Michael killed by the Yanks if that was what had Sara so upset. The only time I had seen anything so horrible was when flies buzzed around my grandfather's coon dog, Cadet, when he died. We had spent a summer in the country before Grandfather passed away, and Cadet got stuck in a trap. It was days before we found the poor dog.

Of course if Pa or Michael were out there, Ma would need my help with my younger brother and sister. This was one of those situations Ma was always telling me about where I needed to act more grown-up.

Taking a deep breath, I tiptoed into the parlor and stood by the window to see if I could hear anything. When I heard Ma gasp, I shut my eyes tight, opened the door, and walked slowly out onto the porch. I had to help her if I could.

Opening one eye at a time, I didn't see Pa or Michael. But there was plenty to upset Sara and Ma. Our soldiers were everywhere—they didn't march in straight lines like they usually did. They straggled by, limping and moaning. Powder burns and blood stained their uniforms. Some of them leaned on each other while they were trying to make it to the battlefield on the other side of town. I saw something strange in their eyes, and I wondered if they could see anything in mine.

In the wagons rolling past, bodies lay stacked on top of each other. Their arms hung over the sides, and bare feet stuck out from the piles. Other soldiers had probably stolen the missing socks and boots. Pa told us in one of his letters that some troops didn't have supplies anymore because the Yankees kept blocking ships, just like they were doing here.

Watching the action in the street, I accidentally looked right into the wide-open eyes of a dead soldier bouncing along on the top of a wagon. I turned my head and fiddled with my braids. I had never seen a sight like this so close before, and I shivered even though it was a hot day in May.

Sara plugged her nose with her fingers. The air did stink, kind of like Cadet had smelled when Grandfather got him loose from the trap and dug his grave. I longed for a cool breeze to blow in from the river and take away the stench.

"Look at them, Ma." James pointed at the men. "They're all dirty and bloody."

"Do you think Pa is with them? Or Michael?" Sara asked.

"Pa's in Virginia. Can't you remember anything? We just got that letter yesterday." James snatched her doll and pretended to throw it in the street. "You're such a baby."

"Give it back!" She reached for his arm.

"James, you better give it back right now," I ordered.

He waved Betty above his head and sneered. "Anna, I don't have to—"

"That's enough," Ma said, and James threw the doll at Sara.

Ma walked down our few steps. I wanted to grab her and hold her with us on the porch. I was afraid she would be swept up with the army and never make it back.

"Excuse me," she said to a soldier in the road. "What's going on here?"

He stopped and tipped his gray cap. As he limped closer, I saw a patch of blood on the knee of his pants. The spot was dark in the middle, like the center of a red rose, and spread out almost in a circle. He wasn't very tall for a man. I could have worn his uniform, and it would have fit better than my dresses from last summer.

He looked down while he spoke. "Ma'am, we're comin' from a terrible battle, up by Black Creek. The Feds had us outnumbered, and we couldn't hold 'em. They're makin' their way here as we speak." He swallowed and wiped his forehead. "We've got orders to head to the trenches and strengthen the forts. Grant's army could try to overtake us as soon as tomorrow mornin'."

"What's he talking about, Anna?" Sara hid behind my skirt.

"There isn't anything to worry about." I turned to her and tucked a loose strand of hair behind her ear. "We've got our cave to hide in," I said, like spending one minute in that cave wasn't as horrible as being buried alive. I didn't want to go back in there—none of us did.

— CHAPTER 3 —
Where's Michael?

When I heard Ma ask the soldier she had stopped, "Have you seen my son, Michael Green?" I listened real close, since she hardly ever mentioned him.

"I don't recall the name, ma'am," the soldier answered. "Is he here in Vicksburg?"

"I hope so." She put her head down.

I went to Ma, placing my hand in hers, and my brother and sister followed. I guessed they didn't want to be far away from us; even though, normally, James and I could go a whole Saturday without seeing each other since I liked reading, and he liked things that got him in trouble.

Sometimes, I didn't care if we lost to the Yankees. Then the war would be over, and Pa and Michael would come back, and our lives would be the way they used to be. Pa and Michael could go to work at their woodworking shop every day while James, Sara, and I went to school. When we all came home, we would eat together the meal that Ma and I cooked, while we listened to Pa's stories or answered questions about what we learned in school. Maybe Pa would tease Michael about the young ladies that visited the shop while Michael worked. We all wondered if he would ever decide on a special one, so we could have a wedding.

I'd get my family together, somehow. I could write letters to General Lee and explain how much we needed our men at home, that there was a battle right here in Vicksburg they could fight. I was good at writing. Ma would be happy I was using my writing to do something good, instead of wasting my time.

I remembered the night before Pa left for the war like it was yesterday. Nellie fixed a big feast as if it was Thanksgiving, and Pa went around telling why he was thankful for each one of us.

Michael was still home then. He didn't leave until two months later when news came that the Blue Bellies were winning. He said he wouldn't have any Yankees telling him whether or not he could own servants. I understood why some slaves wanted to be free with the way their owners treated them. But I guessed George and his family were happy to be with us, and we liked having them here. Although, I wouldn't like being owned by someone. I didn't like how Ma and Pa were bossy sometimes. Maybe one day when things settled down, I'd talk to Noah about it.

All around us, our neighbors lined the streets. Some handed the soldiers food while others yelled, "What are y'all running for? Who's gonna protect us now?"

My heart beat faster as I listened to their angry words. Didn't they realize our men were headed to the trenches, ready to defeat Grant's army when they attacked?

When the sergeant turned to leave, Mrs. Franklin, the nosiest woman in Vicksburg, hurried over. "Young man. Young man," she called breathlessly. She was out of breath whenever doing anything because she was rather plump.

"Yes, ma'am." Again he removed his hat. This time I noticed a thin, pink scar across his forehead.

"Are you boys running scared?" she asked.

"Excuse me, ma'am. I'm not sure what you're askin'," he said.

"I heard the general couldn't keep his men in line. As soon as those Yankee guns appeared, y'all scattered. We're looking at a bunch of yellow-bellies to protect us." Mrs. Franklin threw her hands in the air.

James gritted his teeth. He didn't care for our neighbor, and he probably couldn't stand her insulting a member of the same army our father and brother belonged to. "Listen here, you old busybody," he shouted.

Before he could finish, Ma grabbed his ear.

"Ow! Stop! She hasn't got any right to talk like that." His eyes watered, and he sniffled.

I felt sorry for him because he never learned. Ma didn't let go of my brother's ear no matter how much he squirmed.

Mrs. Franklin's hands went to her hips. She turned away from the soldier. "I declare, Rachel, are you ever going to learn to control that boy of yours?" As she swung back around, she said, "Now young man, like I was saying . . ." But the soldier had already disappeared with the others going by.

"Well, I'll be." This time her hands fiddled with a fine gold comb in her dark hair. "I tell you, Rachel, this is the death of us all."

"I'm scared." Sara hugged her doll with one hand and clung to Ma's apron strings with the other.

Ma frowned. "Mildred, not in front of my children. James will apologize, and then you can be on your way." She released James's ear, which glowed red from her pinch.

He kept his head down, shuffled his feet, and mumbled, "I'm sorry."

I could barely hear him. Ma must not have either because she gave him a light swat on his hand.

"Ow!" He rubbed the spot. He stood up straight, stared into Mrs. Franklin's eyes, and said as loud as he could, "I AM SSSOOORRYY!"

"Well, I never." She huffed and stormed away.

Ma sent James to sit on a stool in the corner of the kitchen. He was used to that. I followed James inside since Ma seemed concerned with the chaos in the road and had forgotten about fixing supper. This would be my chance to start the letter to General Lee.

I found a piece of paper in Pa's desk and grabbed his quill pen and ink bottle. I had only written *Dear General Lee,* when I heard Ma. "Anna! Where did you get to?"

"In here." I put the paper back in the drawer. I wanted it to be a surprise.

"Were you working in your journal? Now? In the middle of our soldiers running for their lives?"

"Well—" I tried to think of an excuse that wouldn't get me in trouble.

She paused and gave me a stern look. "I'm trying to look for your brother." She took a deep breath and added, "Not to mention, supper needs to be finished."

"Yes, ma'am."

She rolled her eyes toward Heaven. "You don't have time to write in your journal now, Anna."

"I wasn't," I said but then stopped trying to explain when she turned away.

When she got to the doorway, she turned back. "Do you understand how important your family is, especially when you're a mother? Your family is the most important. You can never lose sight of that."

"I know, Ma."

"Then come back to the porch to look for Michael. His last letter said he was still in Mississippi. He could be right here in Vicksburg." This time she walked out of the room and left me with tears shining in my eyes.

Michael was important to me. How could she think he wasn't? I remembered the time Michael helped me write my report about President George Washington because I had been sick in bed with a fever and only had one evening to finish it. He knew all about George Washington from when he was in school. There was also the time he carved a grizzly bear out of wood for my fifth birthday. I wanted to see one after Pa told me a story. There weren't any in Vicksburg, so Michael surprised me with the one he made.

I'd show Ma—I'd write that letter and get Pa and Michael to come home. Finally, my writing would do us some good.

On the porch with Ma and Sara, I looked for Michael in the street crowded with wagons, cannons, sheep, mules, horses, and wounded men. The air filled with sounds so full of hurting, Sara and I covered our ears. The smell of gunpowder and body odor stung my nostrils and made my eyes water. It seemed like everyone in Vicksburg stood outside to see what would pass by next.

"Ma, do you see Michael?" Sara asked when one of our neighbors ran out and hugged a soldier in the street.

"No luck yet," she whispered.

We stayed on the porch until the sun went down and never did finish making supper. Nobody seemed hungry anyway. The sight of the bodies and the smell in the air turned my stomach. I glanced at Ma to see if she had any tears, any expression of how awful this was, although I knew better. She didn't believe in showing her emotions—except anger at me.

I bit my bottom lip to keep my feelings inside, but that didn't work. I turned my face, so Ma wouldn't see. After watching the wagons with the dead soldiers passing by, I wondered if I'd ever see my family alive and together again.

— CHAPTER 4 —
Too Quiet

"Anna, wake up!" Sara's voice echoed in our attic room.

I barely opened my eyes and saw her standing at the foot of our bed. "It's still dark out. Go back to sleep."

"I'm not tired." She climbed up near me and knelt down.

Sara didn't usually wake early. None of us did. Ma always had to drag us out of bed, and she hated that. Then we were cranky with one another around the breakfast table—well, except for Pa. He loved the morning, loved to rise before the sun and give the servants their orders before he went to his shop. But Pa wasn't here this morning to make Ma smile.

"I *am* tired." I had stayed up late, writing General Lee's letter. "Go get Ma."

"I'm afraid," she said.

"Afraid of what?" I thought we were getting used to the shelling. Two days had passed since our soldiers had retreated to the battlefield. Since then, the Yankees had fired their cannons day and night, but no shells had come close enough for us to have to hide in the cave. Thank goodness.

"Please, Anna," Sara whined. "I can't go downstairs by myself."

It *was* too quiet and a bit eerie. Were the Yankees sneaking onto the Mississippi's banks while it was still dark? Were they going to climb up Vicksburg's hills and rob us, holding us at gunpoint in our house? Sometimes, I wished I didn't have such a good imagination. Probably the Yanks were just taking a rest before another day of shelling.

"It's stopped." Sara held her breath. "Do you think it's over?"

I closed my eyes, wanting to go back to sleep and forget this whole war.

"Let's wake Ma. I'm hungry," she said.

James's snoring echoed from the other side of a yellowed sheet that served as the only partition between my brother's bed and ours. Ever since our men had signed up with the army, James slept in our room. We moved his bed, pretending that Sara and I were the ones who were afraid, and he would be able to protect us better if he was in our room.

With James's noise, Sara's whining, and all the quiet outside, there was no use going back to sleep. Sara took my hand and pulled me down the stairs into Ma's room before I even had a chance to stretch. Ma was up, dressed in a light blue dress with a white cotton apron tied around her waist. She looked surprised that we were already awake.

"Since the firing's stopped, we've got to get some work done," she said while she twisted her hair into a tight bun. "Sara, wake your brother and tell him to go to the servants' quarters. I need George and Noah tending to the garden while it's safe outside."

Yawning, I sat on the bed while Ma continued. "For goodness sake, Anna, get dressed. We need to make some breakfast."

I knew I'd have to help, that it was my place, but I had planned to spend time writing in my diary first. I wanted to write about the bombs rushing through the sky and destroying some of the buildings in town. One had landed on our school yesterday and shattered the roof.

A cannonball shot through Mr. Adams's front door and stuck in his wall. It flew right past his son's arm, brushing up against his jacket and scorching it. Folks said you could hear his screams all the way down to the river. Mr. Adams charged one cent to see the cannonball, which was about the size of a large grapefruit, wedged into his wall. James snuck in for free and told me about it.

After Sara left to wake James, I started to walk out of the room, but Ma stopped me. "Anna," she said in that certain tone she used when a lecture was coming. She swallowed hard. The quiet in the room was almost worse than the shells screeching in the air.

"Yes, Ma?"

She cleared her throat. "I know you love books and writing in your journal. You're a lot like your pa, and that's a good thing. I love how smart he is and how good he is with numbers. But . . ." She paused to wipe tears from her eyes.

Ma was crying? In front of me?

"I meant what I said about your family being important."

"I know, Ma, it's just—"

She put up her hand to stop me from saying more. "War is here, Anna. It's time for you to start acting like a woman, whether or not you want to. Our men are gone."

"But, they'll come back."

"Yes, and it's up to us to keep our family together and our household running until they do. You can't do that with a pen in your hand and your nose in a book." She looked straight into my eyes. "I don't say this to take away what you love. I say this because I don't want you to lose *who* you love. Now, pray with me for your brother and Pa."

We knelt at the edge of the bed and silently prayed, although I couldn't concentrate. Ma claimed to understand me, but she didn't. I'd find a way to send the letter to General Lee without Ma's help. I wished Pa were home. He always made things better. There was no reason he needed to be in Virginia when there was a war right here in Vicksburg.

In Pa's last letter, he wrote that he hadn't seen any fighting yet in Virginia. He missed us awful and sent his love. He wanted Sara to be brave, and James to act as the man of the house.

"I am the man of the house," James said the rest of the night after he read the letter.

Pa wrote that he had managed to read the Good Book every night, and I should, too. I should start at the beginning and read it to the end. I missed him terribly but understood why it was so important for him to leave us and fight for our land. It wasn't right that the Yanks were trying to bully us.

After a few moments of quiet praying, Ma's clammy hand touched my arm as a signal to go on. I turned to look at her and saw a single tear sliding down her cheek. "Get changed," she whispered.

I rose quickly and left without saying anything. She wouldn't want me to watch her cry.

— CHAPTER 5 —
Cannonball!

James bounded into the house, arms full of sticks, and dropped them in the middle of the kitchen.

"What are you doing now?" Ma asked.

"I'm building a fort. Like the man of the house should." He squatted on the floor and arranged the twigs.

"No you don't. Take those out back. We've got to get these few biscuits made before the cannons start up again." Ma opened the oven door to check on them. We couldn't make too many since we were almost out of flour.

When we cleaned up the flour and sugar spills after the attack a few weeks ago, we tried to save as much as we could. The prices at the General Store were getting higher every day. The shopkeeper raised them because he had fewer and fewer supplies, although some people thought he was just being greedy. Before I put the flour back on the shelf, I could see dirt in the tin—gray and brown specks mixed in with the white.

"Why don't you build your fort around the mouth of our cave since you're the man of the house?" I teased James. "I'm sure that'll protect us from the Yankees."

"Maybe I will." James gathered his twigs.

"Hush up," Ma ordered. "I'm trying to teach your sister how to make a proper breakfast." She wiped beads of sweat from her forehead and smoothed back a few strands of her strawberry blonde hair. She sat down at the table and cracked open three eggs into a bowl.

"Only three eggs for all four of us?" James asked.

Ma gave him a look that told him if he didn't stop complaining right away, his twigs would be out the door, and he'd be in the corner. He picked up his last stick and stomped out.

When I plopped down in the chair next to hers, my dress caught on the back and ripped. The dress was a little tighter this year since I was starting to take the shape of a woman. Now I'd probably have to learn how to sew new clothes for myself if we could afford to buy any material. The calico curtains I had managed to make last winter rustled in the warm breeze blowing in the kitchen. Those curtains were hard enough—I'd never be able to make my own clothes.

"You just tore your dress," Sara announced from her stool in the corner. She never minded her own business.

Ma ignored her and started another lecture. "You're already thirteen years old and could have a husband in a few years, Anna. You have to know how to run a household. You can't count on marrying a rich man who has servants to do everything for you. That's exactly what happened to Nancy Lo—"

A piercing noise cut through the room and drowned out Ma's words. It sounded as if shells were heading right for us, like we were the targets. A terrible feeling came upon me, and I knew we would be hurrying to our cave soon.

My brother ran into the kitchen as a loud explosion sounded in front of our house.

"Stay here," Ma ordered and darted through the parlor to look out the door.

The furniture shook. The windows rattled. When jars, tins, and candleholders clattered to the floor, Sara, James, and I ran into the parlor instead of staying put like Ma wanted. The air filled with a roaring sound that made my head pound like someone was banging a hammer inside. I shoved my hands over my ears, trying to keep out the racket.

"What's going on, Ma? Can you see anything?" I shouted.

"A lot of smoke and dirt and fire," she yelled. Slamming the door, she coughed while trying to speak. "Children, come to me." She waved her hands.

We hurried to a corner in the front room of the house and crouched next to her. She wrapped her arms tightly around us, holding us close to her heart. Sara cried. My breathing was fast, and James held his. I wondered when Ma would say those dreadful words: "To the cave, children." I knew she didn't want to go in there either, but she wanted us to be safe.

The roaring grew closer and closer. Our bodies shook as the bombs hit the ground. "It'll be over soon," I whispered. The Yankees never shot heavily at us for long periods of time, just enough to scare us. But the cannons kept booming and booming and booming. I gritted my teeth and prayed for this horror to end. When I said, "Amen," the loudest boom of all sounded.

"What was that?" James asked. "Those stupid Yankees—"

An explosion in the kitchen cut off his words. Glass shattered; tins and utensils crashed to the floor. It had finally happened. A shell struck our house! James jumped up, but Ma grabbed his arm and made him get back down.

"I want to see what happened," he yelled.

She shook her head and kept a hold of James's arm until he sat down. "No one's going into the kitchen. We'll see the damage later."

I held on tighter to Ma, wishing this was a nightmare. Then she could make it go away like she did when I was younger, when I woke up screaming about a lion Pa had read about or Grandfather's dog coming back to life. She always held me on her lap and rocked me near the attic window until I fell asleep again.

"We have to go to the cave," James said. "Pa would want us to."

"I know." Ma's voice remained low. "Girls, stay crouched down and next to the house."

Sara gripped her doll. "Anna, can you carry me?"

"No, you're too big. We have to hurry. Grab my hand, and let's go."

Ma swung open the front door, and we bolted off the porch to the side of the house. Smoke filled my lungs and stung my eyes. Tears welled up as I coughed and gasped for fresh air. Sara squeezed my hand so hard I expected my fingers to turn blue. We stayed in a line as Ma led us to safety once again.

Shells crackled above our heads and fell a few feet from us. I had a hard time keeping my balance each time they hit. One bomb exploded a few feet from us. I stuck out my arms to block James and Sara. The pieces of the shell landed in front of us. Pa had taught us pieces of a shell landed in front of its explosion.

We made it to our hideout where George and Noah were waiting. I was glad to see them. George took my hand and helped me into the cave. He did the same for Sara and James. Once we were all inside, Noah stood on his tiptoes to stretch a tent-fly across the front opening, and George put one across the back. They probably thought it would help with all those mosquitoes that bit up our arms.

Then our servants stayed outside, near the entrance of the cave. I knew it wasn't proper for them to come in, especially since Pa wasn't here. But I still worried about them. We needed George and Noah, just like we still needed Nellie. We'd be lost without them.

Ma's arms protected us as we stood, silent, in the middle of the cave. Sara was the first to speak. "Mama," she cried. "I dropped my doll."

Ma kissed her forehead. "Hush, darling. We can find her when the shooting stops."

"I've got to get Betty!"

I sat down on the rocking chair and motioned for my sister to climb on my lap. Humming softly, I rocked back and forth while she sobbed. The cannons' blasts competed with my song.

I expected James to call Sara a big baby, but he didn't. "I'll go find it for you," he said. And before anyone had a chance to stop him, he took down the tent-fly and ran out.

"James!" Ma yelled. "No!" She went after him.

Sara and I bolted from our chair and raced over to watch them. Through the smoke and dust, Ma chased after James, but he was too fast. George followed them both. Dust drifted into the cave, making me cough. I couldn't catch my breath. Some shells landed so far away I didn't see them go down. But a few almost hit our house again. When one hit an old tree, it fell, and the limbs broke through the window of our bedroom.

"James!" Ma shouted, but he just kept running.

Sara squeezed me around the waist, making me cough again. I longed for a glass of water to quench my dry mouth, but even more, I longed for Ma and James to come back into the cave. Sara buried her head into my dress as James picked up Betty and held the doll above his head. At the same moment, a shell whistled through the air and headed right towards Ma.

"Ma," I screamed. "Look out!"

It was too late. She didn't move out of the way, and then she fell to the ground. Powder and smoke settled in a haze around her. I heard myself scream and felt my body tremble.

— CHAPTER 6 —
Ma!

James shook Ma real hard, but she didn't move.

"Ma!" I screamed.

I waited and waited for her to move, even just her foot or her hand or her fingers. But she didn't. She just lay there still, too still, with everything else around her moving—tree limbs crashing, smoke swirling, lumber flying.

"Ma, get up!" I yelled again. "Hurry, before another shell comes."

I wanted to run to her and shake her hard, harder than James did—maybe he wasn't strong enough—but my legs felt heavy and wouldn't go. I stayed in the cave as shell after shell fell from the sky.

My brother lay on the ground next to Ma until George picked him up and carried him to the cave. He was moving so slow.

"Hurry up," I yelled. "You have to go and get Ma. She can't move."

George placed James on the floor and said, "Stay here." He walked back to Ma, picked up Betty, and

29

stuffed her in his pocket. Then he gently lifted Ma's limp body from the ground. My heart sank into my stomach like an anchor to the bottom of the river. I knew she was dead before he came back and told us.

When I heard George's words, "I'm sorry, children. Missus Green is passed," I felt like I was outside of my body watching him speak. Was this really happening to me? I was never going to see Ma's smile again or hear her say that family is the most important? My body froze. Maybe if I stayed real still, I could pretend Ma was safe in the cave where she should be.

I bit my lip to keep the tears from coming, trying to keep my feelings inside like Ma taught me. Soon enough I tasted my own blood, and a few tears leaked out. While I sniffled and wiped my eyes on my sleeve, James pounded the floor with his fists—the sound almost louder than the shells.

I took a deep breath and cursed him in my head. *You did this!* But in my heart, I knew James had been trying to help, just like Pa wanted him to.

"Anna, why isn't Ma getting up? What's George doing? Why is James hitting the floor?" Sara's voice rose with each question until she was screeching the words.

I couldn't answer, but I screamed plenty inside my head. *You and your dumb doll! Why did you drop it?*

George said to Noah, "Son, I'm gonna fetch Reverend Lohrs. You wait here. The bombs is still falling."

I couldn't hear exactly what Noah said, but he sounded scared.

"I'se got to go," George said. "Missus Green can't stay here."

As he hurried away, I stared at Ma's limp body lying still near the cave entrance. Blood soaked through her favorite blue dress and drenched her white apron. George had folded her hands together and rested them on her stomach. Noah was standing there and looking at Ma. Tears ran down his face, too. I remembered that day his ma died and the loud sobs that poured from him. Somewhere inside me, I had those, too; but I wouldn't let them out. Ma was not gone yet. A miracle could happen, like in the Good Book. All I had to do was pray. "God, please," I whispered. "We need our ma. Please help us."

I took a couple steps toward her and leaned down to kiss her cheek. Her skin felt cold to me, and her face looked like a stranger's. This wasn't Ma. Ma was pretty, with shiny eyes and thick, strawberry blonde hair. Her cheeks always had a bit of color. I wanted to get as far away from this body as I could with its pale skin.

Sara clutched me so tight around the waist, I could hardly breathe. We crept backwards until we couldn't go any farther, until our backs were against the cave wall. We slid down and sat on the ground.

While we waited for someone to come and help, I held my sister like Ma had just held us in the house. I could still feel her arms around us and her breath on my cheek.

"Stop squeezing so hard," Sara said. "You're hurting me."

"I'm sorry," I whispered.

James got up and stood at the cave's entrance as still as our curtains on a windless, summer day. He usually never stayed in one place longer than grease popping on a hot griddle. That's what Pa said.

A giant sob leaped out of my throat while I thought about Ma lecturing me on getting married and being a good wife. I should have said, "Yes, Ma. I promise to act like a proper woman. I'll do whatever you say." I wouldn't stick my nose in a book or waste my time writing. I'd be right by her side, trying to keep this family together and helping her look for Michael, maybe even going to the battlefield with her.

"Please, Ma, come back to us," I whispered. "I promise to be a good daughter."

Every once in a while, a shell flew through the air, and Sara jumped. I untwisted her braids and ran my fingers through her golden hair until Reverend Lohrs finally arrived. He'd been the Reverend about as long as I'd been alive. He had even baptized me when he first came to town.

"My dear children," he paused and scratched his head, which had just begun to sprout some gray hairs. "I'm so sorry for your loss."

I didn't say anything to the Reverend. He was supposed to believe in miracles. Why didn't he give Ma a chance? Why don't they go get Dr. Franklin?

Instead, he handed Betty back to Sara, and she grabbed her, finally letting go of me. George must have given that stupid doll to him. I should have snatched it and ripped it to pieces. If it wasn't for Betty, Ma would be here.

"Hello, Anna." Reverend Lohrs nodded to me and smiled.

My throat closed, not allowing any words to get through to greet him. I didn't feel like talking to anyone.

He folded his hands and whispered a prayer.

"Amen," Sara said when he finished.

Reverend Lohrs helped us stand and wrapped his strong arms around us. He was much taller than our Pa and had to duck inside the cave, like George. "God is with you," he told us.

I only felt alone.

He continued, "Children, I want you to come and stay with my family tonight. I'll take care of the arrangements for your ma once I get you settled in."

Sara glanced up, her face puffy and streaked. "What's arrangements?"

"What do you think?" James shouted. "Somebody's got to do something with Ma. We can't leave her in the yard forever."

James was so angry. I should've said something and helped Reverend Lohrs, but what? He was the preacher; he could take care of it. Besides, what could I say? Our ma was dead. This wasn't fair, and I didn't understand it.

"This is all Sara's fault," James yelled. "She made me go out there and find her doll."

"I didn't!" Sara moved closer to me.

"Children." Reverend Lohrs put his arm on James's shoulder. "We should prepare to leave." He took my brother to the back of the cave where Sara and I had sat earlier. While the Reverend whispered to him, James covered his face with his hands.

I stood quietly as tears fell down my cheeks. This was it. This was really it. There wasn't going to be a miracle. Dr. Franklin would not be able to save her. Our ma died and left us here alone to take care of ourselves.

Sara took my hand. "Anna, what are you doing?"

I knew what I had to do, what Ma would have wanted. I needed to take care of Sara and James the best I could, even though I didn't know how to do anything well, and we would probably starve. The right thing was to let the Reverend help us until I could clear my mind and think better.

After I lit a candle, I tried to tell Sara what to gather to take with us to the Lohrses, although I wasn't remembering everything. My mind couldn't concentrate on anything for more than a minute. I finally told her, "Just put in things we use every day."

I rummaged through a trunk and found Ma's money jar under a quilt she had sewn last year. The jar used to hold peaches through the winter. But since the Yankees had started this war, Ma had filled it to the top with coins. She used to have paper money in there, too, but had spent the bills on high priced supplies at the General Store. I put the jar and Ma's quilt in a chest to take to the Lohrses. George and Noah would carry our things across town this evening. The shelling usually stopped while the Yankees ate their supper.

When we reached the Reverend's cave, Mrs. Lohrs and her daughter Emily, who was about the same age as Sara, greeted us. A smile lit up Mrs. Lohrs's pretty round face, but her eyes were puffy and red, and I could tell she'd been crying. Ma had helped Mrs. Lohrs with sewing ever since Emily was born. The Reverend's wife had skills like mine when it came to making clothes and blankets.

She hugged us with her plump arms, and I remembered Ma holding us the same way a few hours ago. I pulled away and started unpacking some of our things.

The Lohrses' cave was smaller than ours and crowded with mattresses, a table, and a few chairs. I wondered how the Reverend could bear it. He had to stoop over whenever he stood up. Wooden poles took up even more space in the middle of the room.

"It stinks in here," James said, and not quietly either.

"Hush," I said, even though I agreed. It smelled like a mix of body odor and mold. I figured the Lohrses had been living in their cave for a while, along with all the mosquitoes buzzing around.

I couldn't catch my breath and stepped into the evening air. A gentle breeze rustled the leaves on the branches above my head. I lifted my arms to the sky and stared up at Heaven, wondering if Ma could see me. A shell flew overhead. The Yankees must have finished their supper and couldn't wait to start bombing us again. What if the smoke blocked Ma's view? The stupid bombs. The stupid, horrible, murdering bombs. If only the Yanks would go back home and leave us alone and everything could go back to the way it was. I didn't care why we were fighting. What difference did any of it make? The Yankees already took away my ma, pa, and brother. They might as well take away George and Noah, too.

"Anna," Mrs. Lohrs called. "You better come back in here where it's safe. I've made a small supper."

We crowded around the table, Sara and I sharing the same chair. While Emily said grace, James's elbow kept knocking into me as he fiddled with his fork. I pushed my food back and forth on my plate, not feel-ing much like eating. Sara and James barely touched the food on their plates either. I hoped Mrs. Lohrs wouldn't think we were wasteful. She had cooked the rest of the ham for us, only three small pieces.

After we sat in silence, listening to the Yankees' cannons, Reverend Lohrs said, "We need to let your pa and brother know what happened."

A knot twisted in my stomach. "Maybe we could send them a telegram," I whispered.

He took a bite of his meat. "Grant's destroyed the lines between here and Jackson. We can't get a tele-gram through. You'll have to write letters."

"A letter's gonna take too long," James said.

The Reverend patted my brother's back. "I'll check around and see if there's anything else we can do."

I remembered my letter to General Lee back at our house. I would need to get it soon, especially since it would take so long to reach him. I would have to add more to it, though. Lee needed to know the news about our ma, even though I didn't want to have to write those terrible words. He would just have to let our men come home when he read we were in Vicksburg with-out any mother or father. He couldn't let Pa or Michael stay in the war and risk their lives, too. Then we would have nothing.

— PART 2 —
Separated

— CHAPTER 7 —
Saying Good-bye

The next morning, my body hurt from sleeping on a quilt on the hard floor. I had tossed and turned most of the night. Thoughts of what we would do without Ma filled my head. What would become of James and Sara? I could hardly bake a decent loaf of bread or sew a pair of curtains. I needed help. I needed Pa and Michael.

"Come on children, gather around the table." Mrs. Lohrs interrupted my worrying with a cold breakfast of two strips of bacon and a biscuit. "I'm sorry we don't have much to eat this morning."

"That's all right, ma'am. I'm not too hungry." The thought of eating still turned my stomach. I forced a piece of biscuit down anyway and dreamed of returning home, singing "Bonnie Blue Flag" with Ma, reading stories to Pa, and listening to Michael's dreams of owning his own woodworking shop. I would never complain about having a cooking lesson. I'd listen and work real hard. I would do anything to bring them back.

"Where's the Reverend?" James asked.

"He went down to the store this morning to find out about the telegraph lines." Mrs. Lohrs frowned. "I thought he'd be back before the cannons started up again."

No one said much as we waited. My legs jiggled, and before long, I hit the leg of the table. James's water spilt on his lap. When I hopped up to fetch a rag, I upset the table again, this time spilling Mrs. Lohrs's coffee. "I'm sorry," I said, thinking about the Reverend and wondering when he would return.

He finally came in as we finished breakfast. "I think your brother might be right here, at the battlefield."

We all talked at once. "Michael? Why? Did you see him?"

He motioned for us to be quiet. "I talked to a couple of soldiers when I went downtown this morning." He pulled up a stool and sat with us. "We can send a letter with the courier, and it should reach Michael by tomorrow. The courier takes mail back and forth between the town and the battlefield every night."

"How does he do that?" Sara asked. Her eyes, hazel like mine, opened wide.

"If he feels it's not safe by land, he uses the river. He sneaks down to the shore at dark and gets in his rowboat. Sometimes, he holds on to a piece of lumber and floats through the river. He'll do anything to get people their mail." Reverend Lohrs stood and crossed the room. He removed a few sheets of paper, a quill, and a bottle of ink from a small wooden box. He brought the writing supplies back to the table and placed them in front of me.

"I don't know what to write," I said. This was one of the only times I could ever remember that I didn't feel like writing.

"You have to do it." Sara smiled, showing the gaps where she had lost her baby teeth. "I want to help."

"Me, too," James said.

I took a deep breath. If Ma were here, she would expect me to be the grown-up and write the letter.

"Then, we'll do it together."

After we cleared the breakfast dishes, we decided to write Pa first. I thought of him in a clean, gray uniform, playing cards with the other men he had described in his last letter. Then I imagined him reading our letter and wanting to come home. My hands trembled, but I steadied them enough to write.

> *Dear Pa,*
> *Sara, James, and I have horrible news. We do not know how to tell you this. Ma is dead. A bomb struck her while she searched with James in the backyard for Sara's doll. George helped us get in touch with Reverend Lohrs, and we have been staying in his cave. The Yankees are firing at Vicksburg all day and night. We are scared but trying to be brave. We wish you were here and hope that General Lee will let you come home soon. I am working on a letter for him right now, explaining why he should let you and Michael visit us, at least for a while. By the time you read this, Ma's funeral will be over because this letter will take too long to get to you. But we have good news. Reverend Lohrs told us that Michael is right here with the troops defending Vicksburg. Maybe we will get to be with him soon. Do not worry too much about us. James wanted to tell you he is doing a good job as man of the house.*
> *We miss you and love you,*
> *Anna*

I placed the note in an envelope. Then we wrote the same tragic news to Michael and gave the letters to the Reverend.

When we arrived at the church for Ma's funeral, Sara didn't want to go inside.

"I'm scared, Anna," she whispered and squeezed my hand.

I didn't want to go in either. I remembered Grandfather's funeral, how much everyone had cried, even Pa. Now this was it—our last good-bye to Ma. After today, we'd only visit her grave and see a headstone that listed her name, birthday, and the day she died. And I bet for a while, nothing would mark her resting place. The Yankees probably took the supplies to make Ma's grave marker.

I knew we had to go into the church. People braved the Yankees' shelling to pay their last respects to our ma. We couldn't be the only ones absent.

Picking Sara up, I said quietly, "You can sit real close to me. Everything will be just fine." I held her carefully and tried not to wrinkle her lacy green dress or my navy blue one.

She rested her head on my shoulder as we entered the church with Mrs. Lohrs. Shells had roared through the sanctuary, breaking the beautiful stained-glass windows. Cannonballs splintered the wooden pews, leaving some broken in two or three places. The destruction of this place was a perfect fit for the day. The bombs had destroyed our beautiful Ma and ripped our family apart, splintering our hearts and leaving them broken, too.

Outside, a shell flew through the air, causing me to jump and almost drop Sara. She felt heavier than usual, but not as heavy as the feeling in my chest. At least the Yankees weren't shooting at us too much today, and I was thankful since I wanted Ma to have a nice service and for everyone to be safe.

Sara, James, and I followed Mrs. Lohrs slowly down the aisle. The smell of burning candles filled the room so strongly, James covered his nose with his hand. My eyes darted over the people in the pews. I hoped to spot Michael in the crowd. Hope was one of the only things that kept me going. We hadn't heard from him yet, but I thought maybe my letter could have reached him. It was just like Michael to come to the church and surprise us instead of sending word first.

In the third pew, Mrs. Franklin, our nosy neighbor, sat with her family. She smiled and waved at Mrs. Lohrs but ignored me. I didn't care. Nothing could stand in the way of Ma's day—not the armies and surely not that busybody.

We found our place in the front of the church. Mrs. Lohrs sat down first, and I placed Sara between us on the hard seat, hoping the Reverend's wife would help me comfort her. It was difficult to help Sara when she cried over Ma. I needed strong arms around me, comforting me, but there was no one here to do that. I had to have the strong arms now. James slumped in after me, not meeting my eyes.

The service began with slow organ music playing a sad song, "The Vacant Chair." Then Reverend Lohrs read scriptures and said kind words about Ma. I swallowed hard to keep down the burning in my chest.

I could have been a much better daughter, and James certainly could have been a better son. Is that why this happened? I thought about the time Ma had instructed both of us on picking apples, on how to choose the right ones, how to tell if they were ready or not. Neither of us listened. I was thinking about *Jane Eyre,* and with James, there was no telling what he was thinking about. But when we brought in the basket of apples, we had picked the wrong ones and ruined most of that crop. Ma was furious and sent us both to our room.

There was also the time my bread didn't rise and came out of the oven as hard and flat as a metal pan. And the first time I sewed those calico curtains that hung at our kitchen window. They were lopsided, and Ma had to rip the stitches out and make me start over. Or when Michael and I stayed up all night playing game after game of checkers, trying to see who would be the champion and then fell asleep during the church service the next morning.

But I knew she loved me, James, Michael, and of course, little Sara. Who didn't love Sara? I remember last Christmas when we sat around the fire and listened to Ma share stories of her childhood and how excited she was to get her first doll. I used to love when Ma brushed and braided my hair, even after I was old enough to do it myself. Her hands were so gentle, and she always took time to rub my temples. Her smile shone the brightest whenever I brought home good marks from school or when I finally straightened out the calico curtains.

James tapped my shoulder. "Come on, Anna. What're you waiting for? We have to go outside now."

"Why?" I asked.

"It's over. We have to go to the cemetery." He ran his fingers through his hair.

I wiped my eyes and said a quick prayer, asking God to give me courage and to take care of Ma up in Heaven.

"Anna Green!" Mrs. Franklin shouted.

I pretended not to hear her and walked out the door of the church. "Ma, I promise you," I whispered, "I will act more grown-up, and I will do everything to keep our family together."

Sara grabbed my hand, and we followed the Reverend to the graveyard.

The next day, I waited and waited for a letter from Michael. When I wasn't helping Mrs. Lohrs with any chores, I looked outside, hoping to see the courier. My heart sank when the sun set, and no word came. Pictures of the courier drowning with our letter filled my mind. A sinking feeling clutched my chest until I felt suffocated. And it wasn't only because we had to bury Ma. Would my whole family ever be together again?

— CHAPTER 8 —

Mrs. Franklin's News

While the soldiers were busy eating instead of shooting at us, George took me across town to fetch some more clothes and supplies from our house. He had come to the Lohrses this morning to help the Reverend with a few chores and then help me. Good old George—I knew he was sad because his wife and new-born baby had died, but no one could ever tell. He was just like Ma and never showed his feelings. He always knew the right thing to do. Why couldn't I be more like them?

Pieces of shell lay in the street along with bricks and tree limbs. Loose boards and broken glass covered yards and crushed the grass. I was afraid our house wouldn't be standing when we got there. Bombs had even ripped through bushes, tearing them apart.

While we had a quiet sky, people cooked outside their caves. My stomach rumbled when I smelled the frying bacon. It was the first time since Ma died that I felt hungry. I wondered how much longer we would have bacon or ham or any meat.

Almost every hillside had a cave dug out of it. Nobody wanted to leave Vicksburg and let the Yankees win, so we lived underground instead. I wondered if anybody else, besides me, ever wanted to give up, so our men could come home.

Our neighbor, Mrs. Adams, scrubbed her wash in a large tub on her front porch, just like Ma and me last Saturday. Sara had danced around, singing "Hurrah! Hurrah!" while I rinsed the clothes that Ma rubbed on the washboard. As I blinked back tears, I nodded to Mrs. Adams, so she wouldn't think I was impolite. But I didn't feel like talking to her, especially about the weather or the soldiers or any small thing. How could I talk about unimportant things while my mind was screaming about how much I missed Ma?

"Anna! Anna Green!" someone called. I gritted my teeth when I realized the voice belonged to Mrs. Franklin.

George and I waited for her to catch up.

"Young lady, what're you doing?" she asked. "Crossing town by yourself with that Negro?" She tugged at her petticoat and let out a warm onion-scented breath in my face.

Ma had taught me to always be polite, but I didn't want to be nice to Mrs. Franklin. I imagined saying, "None of your business, you old busybody," like James would have. But instead, I said, "I've got to gather some clothes, and George is helping me."

"Oh, I figured you'd return to get some books or that silly journal you're always writing in." She raised her eyebrows and peered down her long, pointy nose— the only narrow part of her body.

I clenched my fists. "Yes, ma'am, I'll most likely grab those, too." I started on my way.

"My dear." Mrs. Franklin stopped me. "I ran over here to bring you on up to Sky Parlor Hill. There's quite a sight on the river below."

"What happened?"

"Those Yanks were at it again. Trying to get one of their big ships past Vicksburg. But this time our boys were ready for them. We sank the *Cincinnati*."

"Did the Yankees drown?"

"Why yes, some went down with the ship." She squinted her green eyes and looked just like a witch. "Come on, there's a whole crowd up on the hill. It's a perfect place to watch the action." She clutched my wrist with her sweaty hand.

"No thank you, ma'am." I tried to twist free. "I have to get back to watch Sara and James."

"Yes, of course you do. I guess Mrs. Lohrs has told you how much trouble your two siblings are."

I glared at her and yanked my hand free. "No, ma'am?"

"Then I'll be the one to break the news. The Lohrses just can't afford to keep you children, and no one's sure when your daddy and brother will return. And since we have one of the largest and finest caves in all of Vicksburg—you know my husband is such a successful doctor." She paused to catch her breath. "Anyway, Dr. Franklin offered for you and James to stay with us. Ya'll be coming tomorrow."

"What?" I wasn't sure if I heard her right. Why would the Lohrses send us to live with her? They were so kind and loving, and Mrs. Franklin was nothing but a busybody.

"That's right." She winked. "You and James are coming to live with us."

"And Sara?" I whispered, barely able to get enough breath to speak.

"The Lohrses can keep her. She hardly eats anything. And besides she couldn't help me much around the house." Then she grinned although it looked more like an evil sneer. "Or should I say 'cave.'" She waved her hand in front of her face and chuckled at her awful joke.

"I'll have to ask about this."

"Ask all you want, Anna Green. But I'll still see you tomorrow." She showed a mouthful of horse teeth and waddled on her way.

"Sara will not be separated from us," I said and stormed ahead of George. I would not lose any more of my family.

When I reached our house, it was still standing strong. That was one less thing to worry about. The roof over the kitchen was the only place where a cannonball had hit. Once inside, I could still smell smoke and remembered crouching in the corner with Ma while the shells had roared above our heads.

I crept into the kitchen to see the damage. The shell had smashed our table and spread black powder everywhere. My poor calico curtains were torn and stained, lying on the floor. I picked them up and remembered Ma teaching me to hem. Sara had sat right in the corner with a calico piece of cloth, too.

What if Mrs. Franklin was right? What if Sara was staying with the Lohrses? I had to find my journal with General Lee's letter in it. I had to start doing something for my family instead of feeling sorry for myself.

Holding the curtains, I ran up to the attic and saw our broken bedroom window. I had forgotten how the cannonballs had knocked over my favorite tree. Dust covered the floor, the beds, and even Sara's little stool. I placed the curtains on the floor, then knelt on them to get my journal from under the bed. When I finally reached it, I flipped through the pages until I found the letter.

> *Dear General Lee,*
> *I have some very important business to discuss with you. My father, Paul Green, and my brother, Michael Green, are soldiers in your army. As you are aware, sir, we are having a battle right here in Vicksburg, Mississippi. Grant is bombing us, and his troops are fighting our soldiers on the battlefield on the other side of town. My six-year-old sister, eleven-year-old brother, my mother, and I are trying to survive with the help of two servants. We had to escape to the cave behind our house when the bombing became too heavy. I know my father and brother would be proud to protect their own city and family from falling into the hands of the Yankees.*

I had stopped writing because I didn't know quite how to ask a general to send his soldiers to another place. I dreaded having to tell Lee about Ma, but I figured I would need to soon.

I stuffed the letter in my sleeve where most young ladies kept their handkerchiefs. Then I read a poem in my journal that I had written about James titled, "Oh What a Rotten Brother." He had made me so angry when I wrote it and deserved every word of that poem.

I had burst into tears one morning because I didn't want to go to school. James overheard me telling my schoolmates a few days earlier that Matthew McDonald was handsome. The next day, during arithmetic lessons, my rotten brother stood on his chair and announced, "Anna Green loves Matthew McDonald. I heard her say so."

I couldn't ever face Matthew again. I cried and cried and begged Ma not to send me to school. All she said was, "A proper lady keeps her strong emotions to herself. She prays for strength and asks God to relieve her suffering. "

"God couldn't relieve this unless he made me disappear," I had answered and got sent to bed.

After Ma had forced me to go to school and I spent the day hiding behind my schoolbooks, I hurried home and went straight to my room.

Pa came in. "I'll get you something, so you can express your feelings but still keep your ma happy." A few days later he gave me a brown leather book full of blank pages, two quills, and a bottle of ink. And that was when I wrote the poem about James.

Even though he had made me so miserable, I wanted to climb inside my journal and relive those days when we were all together. I would do anything to go back, anything.

Plopping down on the mattress, I sent up a puff of dust. I found a blank page near the end of the book, dipped my quill in the ink, and scribbled.

Ma, I miss you very much. I think about you every day and pray you are safe in Heaven. What are we supposed to do without you? It has been all right staying with the Lohrses. But it is crowded, and James gets restless. Still, I thought we could manage there. They are kind, and Mrs.

Lohrs reminds me of you. But, what about Mrs. Franklin? I can not stand her and will not last a day. She does not care about anyone but herself. You should have heard her. She is horrible. Everyone wants to separate us. James, Sara, and I should be together. Pa and Michael should be with us. I know you probably think I should bring Sara and James back here and live on our own. I am not as brave or strong as you, and I did not listen close enough to all your lectures. I am sorry, Ma. I am so sorry, but we would starve to death with my cooking and have no clothes to wear after we outgrew these. I could not face Pa or Michael ever again if I let something happen to James or Sara. But I promise you this, I will find a way to keep us together. I will work hard to find Michael. I will write letter after letter after letter to General Lee until he lets Pa come home. Then we will all be here together to protect one another, just like you tried to protect James from the shells that day. I miss you, Ma.

I put my pen on the bed and buried my head in my hands, finally allowing myself to cry, to sob, to yell and scream—without worrying about being strong for Sara and James or worrying about being a proper lady. I lost myself in the sobs coming from my soul.

Teardrops fell onto my page, smudging a few words. I laid the journal open on my bed to dry.

"Miss Green," George called. "You best hurry. Them bombs'll be startin' soon."

I rushed around to gather a few more things we would need and found my favorite hairbrush—the one Ma used to brush my knotted hair in the morning. Hurrying to the stairs, I accidentally knocked over the inkbottle as the first cannon fired.

"Miss Green, come on!" George yelled again.

When George grabbed my hand, I tried to tell him I left my journal on the bed, but he didn't hear above the shelling. At least I had the general's letter. I took it from my sleeve and grasped it as tight as I could before we headed out into the battle.

— CHAPTER 9 —
Questions and Answers

"You and James are coming to live with us." Mrs. Franklin's words repeated in my mind while I followed George. She had to be wrong. I rushed ahead of him, anxious to prove that the old busybody was also a big, fat liar.

By the time I reached the Reverend's house, I was running to the cave with General Lee's letter still in my hand. I bolted in, out of breath, but managed, "Mrs. Lohrs," before I slumped against the table.

"My goodness, what's the matter?" Mrs. Lohrs placed her embroidery on her lap.

It probably wasn't right to just come out and confront her, since she was my elder and the Reverend's wife, but I needed to know. This was about my family, and Ma said family was the most important. I said a quick prayer so God would understand why I had to question her.

"I saw Mrs. Franklin on my way home." I crossed my arms.

"Yes, dear?" Her big, brown eyes had dark circles underneath, and she looked as tired as I felt.

"She said James and I were going to live with her tomorrow. Is she correct?"

James sprang up. "What did you say?"

"No," Sara said.

"Is Sara staying here with us?" Emily asked, smiling—the only person smiling in the room.

Mrs. Lohrs laid down her sewing and looked into each of our faces. "I'm sorry, Anna. But Mrs. Franklin was correct. I wanted to tell you myself."

"Then why didn't you?" James asked.

She motioned for us to gather around her. Sara put her face in her hands, my brother turned his back, and I stared at my feet.

"Why do they have to go?" Sara's hands muffled her words. "I can't stay here without them."

"Mrs. Franklin said we bothered the Lohrses and spent all their money," I mumbled and looked at Mrs. Lohrs. "Is that true? We have money." I went to our chest, threw down the letter, and reached under the clothes for Ma's jar of coins. "Here." I tried to hand it to her. "We've got more, too. Our grandfather left us money when he died."

She waved her hands. "I won't take that. We love having y'all here. But the Franklins are better able to make you comfortable. I know sometimes she can be a little bossy, but her heart is in the right place. Dr. Franklin offered to help out until your pa returns. The Reverend thought it would be best if Sara remained here and could play with Emily. The days are long for such little children."

"The days are long for me, also," I said. "Do you know what it's like—" and then I stopped. What was I going to say? Do you know what it's like to have a horrible pressure in your chest making it almost impossible to breathe? Or missing someone so much that you beg God for sleep, and in that sleep beg for dreams of that person?

I threw the money jar back in with our clothes.

"Anna," Mrs. Lohrs began, but I put up my hand to stop her.

"Sara needs to be with us," I said.

Mrs. Lohrs put her head down. "I'm sorry, but Mrs. Franklin said they couldn't take all three of you. It'll just be for a little while. And the Yankees won't be shelling us forever. We'll get out of these caves and into our homes. The prices at the General Store will go down and . . ."

Blocking out her words, I turned away and rustled through the trunk until I found the Good Book. I sat in the chair by Mrs. Lohrs's silver candlesticks, opened the book, and tried to read. But I couldn't concentrate on the words. The shells started falling more often, shaking the candles, so Mrs. Lohrs blew them out. I kept thinking about Mrs. Franklin. Living with her would be worse than being a prisoner of the Yankees. Living without Sara and Ma and Michael and Pa would be even worse than that.

My head ached, feeling like it was on fire. I put the Bible on my lap and closed my eyes. Memories of my family laughing and singing on Sara's last birthday raced through my head. The pressure in my chest grew so unbearable I opened my eyes and shook my head. I wanted to be free from my memories, like Vicksburg wanted to be free from the Yankees.

— CHAPTER 10 —
New Home

"Do you think Michael's alive?" James whispered.

I didn't answer. I didn't want to think about anything but spreading a quilt on the floor and getting some sleep. It already felt like we'd been at the Franklins' cave forever, but this was only our second night. Four man-made rooms in this cave weren't enough to get away from Mrs. Franklin.

She and Dr. Franklin slept in the biggest room completely decorated with a nightstand and lantern, pastel quilt for their huge mattress, and painted portraits of her family leaning against the walls. Their twelve-year-old son, Stuart, who behaved as terribly as his ma, slept with them. She gave us the smallest room, with no mattress, of course. We slept on a quilt and pallet on the floor. James snored every night just as loudly as if we were sleeping in our bedroom, and Ma was still alive. How could he rest so soundly when everything was so wrong?

In the other room, Molly, the Franklins' oldest, slept with her baby boy, Peter. She had shiny brown hair that she wore in a bun, and the skinniest waist I ever saw on anyone besides Sara. I liked Molly and was thankful she was here with us, but she hardly ever smiled. Her husband had joined the army and hadn't sent her one letter yet. I knew how she felt, waiting and waiting for a letter that wasn't coming, except Molly had a sick baby to worry about, too.

But a very, very small part of me was a little excited to be living with Mrs. Franklin, only because I wanted to see her nephew, Albert. He was handsome and kind. The chance for visitors in the middle of the bombings was slim. Besides, I wanted him to stay safe in his own cave with his ma and sisters. Families needed to be together.

James spoke louder. "Anna, did you hear me? Do you think Michael's alive?"

"I don't know." I had imagined the reasons Michael hadn't written us—maybe he wasn't in Vicksburg anymore, maybe the courier couldn't find him in the middle of the fighting, or worse, maybe my brother was dead. I was too tired and worried to discuss this with James. "Be quiet before Mrs. Franklin scolds us for waking her up."

"You think I care about—"

"I hear you children in there!" Mrs. Franklin yelled. "Y'all get quiet right now before you wake Molly and the baby. The poor little soul needs his rest."

"We're sorry, ma'am," I said.

"We're not either," my brother whispered.

"What's that?" She had ears like a jackrabbit.

"Nothing, ma'am. We're having trouble getting settled tonight." I motioned for James to lie down.

"Come on, let's get some sleep. We need to be on our best behavior so we can be together with Sara soon."

The cannons started up again. I thought a person might eventually get used to the noise of the Yankees' firing at night, just like we did with the crickets' chirping. But since Ma died, it was hard to get used to anything. I wished I had cotton to block out the shells' screeching and James's pestering.

"What'd you go and say we're sorry for?" he said.

I rolled away from him, and he kicked my leg.

I gritted my teeth to keep from kicking him back and starting our own battle. "We have to live here, and I'm making the best of it." I turned on my side to face him. "What do you want me to do?"

"I want you to take us home! Then Sara will be with us."

"I can't do that, James." I rolled away from him. Besides, what did he know? I could never take care of James and Sara and the meals and the wash and everything else like Ma did. This was all James's fault anyway, and he should just hush up and live with it. He was the one who had run out of the cave to fetch Sara's doll.

At least Reverend Lohrs had taken my letter to send to General Lee before he brought us to the Franklins yesterday. I had finally figured out what to say at the end. I asked the general if he could spare two of his men, Pa and Michael, to send to Vicksburg. I just put one sentence about Ma. It was all I could manage.

Soon enough, I hoped we wouldn't have to worry about being separated from Sara or being quiet for

Mrs. Franklin. Pa and Michael would be back, and then, I would know everyone was safe. The Yankees would stop bombing us, and maybe even this aching in my chest would ease up.

In the morning, Baby Peter's cries woke me. I rubbed the sleep out of my eyes and saw the cave dark as usual. A streak of morning light came in from the back exit, which always heated the cave. By the afternoon, it would be warm and stuffy, and I wouldn't be able to breathe inside. While James slept, I changed into a school dress, braided my hair, and went into the other room. Mrs. Franklin swatted mosquitoes and hovered over Molly, who was slowly rocking her son. They reminded me of when I used to stand next to Ma while she rocked Sara to sleep when she was a baby.

Molly greeted me over her baby's screaming. "Good morning, Anna."

"Good morning."

Mrs. Franklin wasted no time barking an order. "Anna, you need to help Olivia make the coffee."

The smell of smoke filled the cave, so I knew her house servant, Olivia, had already started a fire outside. I was sure she had it all taken care of and didn't need me in her way. Olivia had been a slave for a long time—probably her whole life, almost thirty years, I'd guess.

"I'm not too good at making coffee," I told Mrs. Franklin.

"No excuses." She snatched her red-faced grandson from Molly's arms and paced back and forth. "It's unfortunate that Dr. Franklin used the last of the grounds yesterday. And there's none to be had in Vicksburg, unless you're a member of the blasted army.

So, you'll have to use those acorns in the jar on the shelf."

I'd helped Mrs. Lohrs prepare acorn coffee for the Reverend just the other day. We had roasted some acorns over a fire and smashed them into tiny bits as a substitute for the grounds. Then we strained the boiling water through, and the liquid looked like coffee. I bet it didn't taste anything like real coffee because it didn't smell nearly as good as Pa's used to.

While Olivia and I made the acorn drink, Baby Peter screamed. Dr. Franklin finally came into the room, looking like he just woke up. He had been out late visiting patients. Somehow James slept right through the noise.

"I think we better take little Peter over to the Balfour place today." The doctor ran his fingers through his dark hair, which was starting to turn gray on his sideburns.

"Why?" Molly asked.

Her father took the child from his wife and lowered himself into a chair, cradling his grandson in his arms. "Their place has been converted to a hospital for wounded soldiers, remember? Peter doesn't seem to be getting well, sweetheart, and I'd like to discuss it with someone else."

"I want to go with you." Molly stood and reached for her bonnet.

Her mother stopped her. "Now just hold on here a minute. Nobody's going anywhere without me, and surely not until we've had some breakfast. Anna, are you finished yet?" She shooed Molly over by the doctor, and they both sat to the table. She kissed her daughter on the cheek and patted her husband's shoulder.

In spite of how she treated James and me, I could tell Mrs. Franklin really loved her family. It made me miss Ma even more—I had no mother to kiss me on the cheek, and Pa no longer had a wife to pat his shoulder to calm him down. Why did this happen?

"Anna," Mrs. Franklin barked. "I asked if you and Olivia were finished with breakfast yet?"

"Yes, ma'am." I plopped a china teacup in front of each of them and splashed some acorn coffee from the kettle into each.

"Anna, you are being quite careless with my china." Mrs. Franklin wanted to use only her best dishes and pretend we weren't in the middle of a war. Olivia followed close behind me with a matching plate for each.

"Stuart!" Mrs. Franklin shouted in my ear. "Stuart! Come and eat."

As I served some day old cornbread, cold ham, and the last of the peaches, Stuart trudged from his room and fell into his chair. I tried not to show how much he annoyed me—he was a year younger and just plain stupid.

"Anna, sit down here and get yourself something to eat," Mrs. Franklin demanded. "Is your brother still in bed? At this hour?"

"Yes—"

"This coffee's awful!" Stuart interrupted. "I ain't drinking it."

Still holding little Peter, Dr. Franklin took a sip from his steaming cup. "It is quite bitter."

I didn't know how they were drinking it while it was still so hot. Mrs. Franklin glared at me, then turned her eyes toward Olivia, who was busy mixing something in a bowl. After she sipped it, she placed it calmly on the large oak table and said, "This is the worst drink I've ever had." She took a deep breath and yelled, "Olivia!" even though she was only a few feet away.

Olivia hurried over, keeping her head down. "Yes, ma'am."

"Take this coffee," Mrs. Franklin ordered.

Just then Baby Peter screamed louder than he had all morning, and Dr. Franklin stood up to pace back and forth with him. Molly followed her pa, singing a quiet lullaby and looking more nervous than ever. When Olivia reached for the coffee cup, Mrs. Franklin glanced at her husband to see if he was watching, and then she poured the acorn drink onto her servant's hand.

Olivia bit her lip and shook her hand like she was trying to shake off the heat. Tears welled in her eyes, but she didn't risk letting them out. She looked like me when I used to hide my crying from Ma. Then Olivia wrapped her hand in her apron and grabbed the coffee cup with the other hand.

"You need to be more careful, girl. You might put that hand in some cool water. Although the coffee wasn't that hot." Mrs. Franklin stared at her, like she was daring Olivia to say something.

"Yes, ma'am." She turned away to start cleaning up breakfast.

I couldn't believe what I had seen. Ma and Pa would never treat our servants like that. "Dr. Franklin, your wife just—"

"Anna, if you get the washing finished today, maybe you can go visit Sara at suppertime. Even bring her over here to spend a night in our cave." Mrs.

Franklin reached across the table to take another piece of cornbread. "Now what were you saying, dear?"

I knew exactly what she was getting at. If I kept quiet, she'd let me see Sara today.

"Yes, ma'am." I sounded just like one of her servants. Baby Peter's cries became whimpers, and Molly sat back down at the table. "We can try something different to make coffee with tomorrow, Mother. Lizzie Tucker said they've been using chicory."

"No matter." Mrs. Franklin waved her hand as if the poor tasting coffee was no big deal. Olivia probably wanted to try something different like Molly suggested and save her other hand.

James finally stumbled into the room, wiping sleep out of his eyes. I smiled in spite of myself, thinking about how Ma always nagged us to get out of bed, and one time even poured water over James's head.

"Finally up, young man?" Mrs. Franklin raised her eyebrows and stared down her pointy nose at my brother. "I'd say you won't be able to get all your chores done before it gets dark tonight if you don't start getting up earlier. We have so much to do because of this blasted war and the constant shelling."

"Mildred, let the boy wake up a little first," Dr. Franklin said.

"Dear." She batted her eyelashes at her husband. "The soap's not going to be made by itself, the vegetables certainly aren't going to pick themselves, and I do wish Peter was old enough to make his own clothes."

Dr. Franklin kissed her on the cheek while he patted Baby Peter's back. "Point taken."

James reached for a piece of ham and gobbled it, using only his hands and no manners.

She shook her finger at my brother. "James Green, we do not eat like animals, even if we are living underground like them."

I couldn't believe she was comparing this cave to a rabbit burrow or snake hole. She had everything in here—expensive rugs, crystal vases, even landscape portraits, and they were probably carried from her house by her poor servants.

My brother paid no attention and kept right on chomping his breakfast.

She didn't give up easily. "The first thing I'll have you do this morning, James, is clean up the debris in our backyard. Why, Gabe almost tripped and fell."

James took a big bite of his ham and with food still in his mouth, he said, "Do it yourself, you old witch."

"Gabe!" The old witch slammed her hand on the table. "Did you hear what he called me? Do something!"

"Son, you will go back to your room without any more breakfast," Dr. Franklin commanded.

James stuck out his tongue, scooted back his chair so it scraped against the wood, sending chills down my spine, and stomped out of the room. Why did he have to be so impossible?

Mrs. Franklin rose from the table and grabbed her bonnet from the hat rack by the cave's entrance before she turned to me. "I guess your brother doesn't care too much about seeing Sara today."

"Mildred," Dr. Franklin scolded. "It isn't the girl's fault. Besides, their ma—"

"Oh, I was just teasing." She tied her bonnet. "Doesn't anyone have a sense of humor anymore?"

— CHAPTER 11 —
Bravery

When everyone finished breakfast and got ready to leave, I snuck some food in my pocket for James.

"Mother," Stuart said. "I wanna go. It's boring here, and I ain't staying with her!" He pointed at me.

Mrs. Franklin wrapped Baby Peter in a blanket despite the hot day. "I don't have time to worry about you getting into any mischief over there. Stay here and keep an eye on things for me. Olivia, make certain you and the other servants tend to the outside work this morning while the bombing's stopped." She patted her grandson's back to quiet him down. "Anna, be a good girl and get our washing done, and I want your brother to boil water for drinking after he cleans up the yard."

I nodded but didn't speak to her. If I could, I wouldn't talk to her for the rest of my life. I was glad to see them leave, although I did feel sorry for Baby Peter.

Mrs. Franklin was right about the skies being quiet. Sometimes the two armies agreed to stop firing to bury their dead. If they didn't, the stink of the bodies made them too sick to fight. I wondered if the soldiers dug graves for their friends, or if the dead men had any funeral services before they were buried. I couldn't remember anything about Ma's service, but at least I had the chance to say good-bye. It didn't seem fair that these soldiers died without having a proper funeral with their families. I prayed that wouldn't happen to Michael or Pa.

"James, James!" Stuart called as soon as his family left.

My brother hurried from our room. "What do you want?"

"I got a secret collection."

"So what." James crossed his arms.

"So what? You won't say that when I show you what I got." Stuart left the cave for a few minutes. When he returned, he carried an armload of metal pieces left over after the shells exploded.

I jumped back and almost ran outdoors when he threw them down on the kitchen table. Stuart wasn't very smart, and I figured he might have picked up some scraps that could go off.

"Y'all are a bunch of babies," he said. "These ain't gonna go off."

"Where'd you get those?" James asked.

"I picked them up in the yard. I can make them into a pyramid." Stuart arranged the pieces on the table.

"You're a lunatic," I said. "You don't know if they'll go off or not."

"These are just pieces left after the shells explode. Nothing's gonna happen." He snatched up a jagged piece about the size of his hand and waved it at us.

James headed toward the pile.

"What're you doing?" I asked. "Stay here."

He ignored me and touched the pile of scraps.

"James, don't!" I cried.

"You're so bossy, Anna." He turned to Stuart. "Go outside and show me which ones are safe."

"No." I put my hands on my hips and for a moment felt like Ma. "Mrs. Franklin wants you to boil some water for drinking."

"But first she wants me to clean up the yard." My brother, the traitor, laughed and joked with Stuart on his way out of the cave.

I gathered the mounds of dirty clothes, along with a washboard and bar of soap, and carried them outside. Olivia had filled two tubs with water and heated them a bit over the fire. No one seemed to have done any washing in weeks, and I figured I'd still be working by moonlight.

While I scrubbed lye soap on one of Mrs. Franklin's dresses, I stared at her house. With two stories and a cellar, it was at least three times bigger than ours. I liked the green shutters around her windows and thought about my own house— how plain the windows probably looked. Our house was built from red brick also, but two chimneys towered above the Franklins' roof. She didn't deserve to live in such a pretty place.

I rubbed her dress harder and harder on the washboard. Why couldn't I just do our own chores in our own cave? Maybe James was right. Maybe we could go home. I closed my eyes and imagined what it would be like, but instead, all I could see was Ma's body in the grass and hear her telling me I didn't knead the bread dough right and didn't sew the stitches straight enough. I wasn't ready to be on my own. Ma knew that, but she left me anyway.

"You're a liar," James yelled at Stuart.

I couldn't quite make out Stuart's response, but it wasn't filled with proper words. Soon enough, James sprinted over to where I worked and tumbled on his back. I didn't tell him I had saved some food from breakfast since I was still mad at him. So much for him acting like a man.

His stomach rumbled loud enough the troops probably heard it on the battlefield, and I threw the piece of ham and day old cornbread at his head. He snatched it and gobbled down the meat first.

"What was that all about?" I rinsed the dress in the clean tub of water.

James plucked a blade of grass and put it in his mouth. "Why does our pa have to be fighting in the war, and Stuart's is still right here with his family?"

I wrung the dress to get rid of the extra water and then shook it out. "Stuart's father is helping out in another way—at the hospital. Our pa can't do that, so he's fighting for our land."

"Reverend Lohrs is home."

"What are you getting at, James?" I got up from my stool and hung the dress on the clothesline between the cave and the Franklins' mansion.

"Nothing. I hate the Yankees." He chewed on the grass. "I just wish Pa were here."

"Me too." I was proud of Pa and Michael for risking their lives, and they did need our support. "Don't let Stuart bother you. He doesn't know what he's talking about."

James rested on his elbows. "How 'bout this? Stuart said his ma is giving food to a couple of Yanks without anyone else knowing it."

"Stuart's a liar. She doesn't have that much food. Besides, why wouldn't he tell his pa if he's telling you?" I sat back down on my stool and picked up Stuart's pants.

"I said the same thing, and he said she gives him toys and candy, so he won't tell."

I laughed out loud. "Who has extra toys and candy? You can't believe him."

"I'm gonna find out if it's true; then we'll have to go home. We can't live with a traitor." James turned over on his back again with his arms above his head. "You shouldn't be doing their washing. Ma wouldn't have ever wanted to see you working like that for the old busybody."

It was true. But, I couldn't worry about what Ma would have wanted. I had to keep James and Sara safe until we found Michael and could get Pa home. It would be impossible to live if both our parents were dead. Wouldn't it?

Thinking about what to say to James, I scrubbed the knee on the pants as hard as I could, but the grass stain wouldn't budge. "Mrs. Franklin's letting us live here for free, you know. The least we can do is help out."

"We could go back home," James said. "Maybe I will."

I ignored him and kept washing. I'd already made my mind up about going home.

"How come you haven't been writing in your stupid journal?" He chomped on his cornbread while he talked, and crumbs flew out of his mouth.

"Things are different."

He sat up and stared at me. "Like what?"

I knew James was trying to start an argument, but I couldn't help answering him anyway. "How can you be so dumb? We were just talking about it." I threw the pants into the tub and spilled water over the sides and onto my shoes. "Everything's different." Swallowing hard, I whispered, "Ma's dead, Sara's living with the Lohrses, and our men are gone."

"I'm still here."

I rolled my eyes at him. "Of course you are, James. What was I thinking?" I picked up the pants again. "Besides, I left my journal at home."

"Why don't you go get it?"

I told myself to ignore his questions, but I didn't want him to have the last word. "I'm not going all the way across town by myself, and I've got this work to do. I'm sure Mrs. Franklin wouldn't let me anyway."

He was awful quiet, and I knew what ideas were stirring in his mind. "James, you better not leave without permission. Your bravery got us into this mess to begin with." As soon as those words were out of my mouth, I regretted them.

He turned away from me and shrugged his shoulders like what I said didn't bother him. But the way he pulled his knees close to his body and hugged them with his arms, I knew it did.

"Look, I'm sorry. I just don't really need to be writing right now. I've got other things to concentrate on."

He rested his chin on his kneecap.

"Did you hear me?" I asked.

He got up and strolled into the cave without saying anything or even looking at me. My heart beat
faster, and I wondered what he was going to do.
I stood to go after him just as a Yankee shell flew
over my head again. But it sailed away. Before the shelling grew any worse, I grabbed what wash I could carry
and ran inside the cave, leaving the tubs of water outside. I wondered what would happen if a shell landed
in one, and it blew apart with pieces of wood scatter-
ing everywhere. Then maybe I wouldn't have to do any
more of the washing, although Mrs. Franklin would find
a harder way for me to do it.

When the Franklins came home, Sara was with
them, but Molly and Baby Peter weren't. By the look on
Mrs. Franklin's tear-stained face, I guessed Molly must
have stayed at the hospital with her son.

The doctor held Sara's hand as they walked into
the cave. I ran to her and picked her up, covering her
with kisses while James pulled her braids.

"He's just sore at me," I told Sara.

Mrs. Franklin wiped her eyes with a lacy handkerchief. "Now, Anna, Sara's only going to be able to stay
for supper."

"You said she could spend the night."

"I spoke out of turn. Mrs. Lohrs insisted she return after she finishes eating."

I looked to Dr. Franklin, but he didn't meet my
gaze. His wife was fibbing, I knew she was. She was
taking out her unhappiness on us.

I took Sara's hand. "Then I'll be too busy playing
to help out with supper tonight." I led her into our
room, and James sulked behind.

"You'll be with us soon, Sara, I promise." I retied the bows on the end of her braids. Then I took my hairbrush and fixed her bangs, just like Ma would have. Sometimes on cold winter nights when we used to sit around the fire, Ma would let us fix her hair. One time, we used thirty hairpins, almost every one she owned.

"You know, Sara." James knelt in front of her. "We could all be together now if Anna would just take us home."

Sara smiled at me, and I shook my head no. "James doesn't know what he's talking about." Sometimes he made me so mad that I wanted to push him over and stomp on him. Instead, I took a deep breath and acted like Ma would have wanted. "Anyway, let's play marbles." I rustled around in our chest to find Michael's marbles. I decided right then and there I would let James win, just like Michael used to always let me win, so my little brother would stop being such a nuisance.

After our game, we ate a quiet supper before Dr. Franklin took Sara back to the Lohrses. My heart felt like a hole had been cut out of it, and nothing could fill it. I had to think of a way to protect Sara and keep her with James and me. For every idea I thought of, I thought of a reason why it wouldn't work. Mostly because Mrs. Franklin was so unpredictable.

But my family was the most important thing to me, and I wouldn't stop until I figured out a way for us to be safe and together.

I imagined Pa and Michael home, all us Greens sitting around the table, eating a ham that I had cooked. Olivia served us beans from a china bowl because Pa made some bargain with Dr. Franklin to get her away from Mrs. Franklin. The only thing ruining this scene was Ma's empty chair.

Tired from the day's activity, I fell asleep in spite of the aching in my chest. I dreamed of Ma. She was wearing a white flowing gown with her strawberry blonde hair resting on her shoulders, instead of in a tight bun. A light shone around her, and she led me into Mrs. Franklin's sleeping room. Ma told the old busybody that she ought to be ashamed of herself for treating us so poorly. She forced her to kneel down and apologize to me.

When I awoke in the morning, a warm feeling ran through my body to the tips of my toes until I felt the quilt next to me. James was gone.

— Chapter 12 —
Fire Downtown

I heard the courthouse bell ring twelve times while I set the table, which meant I'd been worrying about James all morning. I had decided he must have gone to get my journal. But when Mrs. Franklin informed me that her husband, Olivia, and the other servants had left to help put out a fire at the general store, I figured he probably overheard Dr. Franklin talking about the fire and followed him downtown. He always wanted to be in the middle of everything, trying to prove that he was a man.

It seemed like more shells than ever had exploded this morning. What would I do if something happened to James? He made me loony, but I wanted him to be safe, to be here with me. I couldn't stand to think of him being gone forever like Ma. Pressure built up in my chest until I wanted to explode. How would I ever explain to Pa that I had managed to lose both Sara and James?

Mrs. Franklin rocked in her chair, blowing her nose and sounding like a horn out of tune. She was too concerned about her own problems to notice James's absence. She probably thought he was busy doing a chore somewhere.

She had cried off and on ever since they returned from the Balfour house yesterday. Dr. Franklin reported Baby Peter had caught diphtheria, which affected his nose and throat. Molly stayed at the hospital to help her son and work with the wounded soldiers, too. The doctor said that being in a cave wouldn't help Peter with his breathing.

"Anna, bring me a drink of water," Mrs. Franklin demanded. "I feel miserable, with my worries over my family and all these mosquitoes. I need my fan. It's hot enough in here to fry an egg on this table."

"Yes, ma'am." It was hard to concentrate on her with my worries over my own family. I paced back and forth, not really looking for the fan, just thinking about James.

She bossed me some more while she fanned herself with her hand, stopping only to swat a mosquito. "And you'll have to fix my plate and bring it to my rocker. I'm much too tired and upset to come to the table to eat with you children."

"Yes, ma'am," I answered again. I prepared her plate with one strip of bacon, a few slices of cucumber, and a hunk of pea bread, another substitute like the acorn coffee. We were running low on cornmeal, so we ground up peas and used the powder along with the cornmeal to make bread.

After I finished helping with dinner, I decided to go look for James. I couldn't stand another minute in this cave, waiting for him to come back. I'd wait for the right moment and slip out.

"Stuart, it's time to eat," Mrs. Franklin said when I handed her the plate of food.

"I'm busy." He sat on the ground and played with marbles that looked an awful lot like Michael's. I'd have to worry about that later.

"You'll come now, Stuart, or you won't eat." Mrs. Franklin took a huge chunk out of her pea bread.

He kicked the marbles and watched them scatter around the room. I imagined his ma falling on one later and smiled.

Stuart and I sat down to the table. "Where's James?" he asked before taking a bite of the bread.

I choked on my food and waited for Mrs. Franklin to question me where James was. But before she even noticed what her rotten son had said, he started complaining. "This bread ain't done."

Mrs. Franklin took another bite. "That's just the way it tastes, Stuart. The cornmeal bakes faster than the pea meal. Just another hardship we must suffer at the hands of the Yankees." She blew her nose into her handkerchief again.

Stuart took the bacon off my plate and replaced it with his bread.

"You can't do that." I switched them back.

"Mother, Anna's touching my food," he shouted.

"Hush up right now, both of you." She fanned herself furiously between bites of her dinner.

He started to swap the food again but stopped when his pa staggered in. Soot covered Dr. Franklin's face, clothes, and bare skin. Water soaked his pants and shirt. He looked as horrible as some of the wounded soldiers I had seen in the wagons a few weeks ago. And he smelled like his clothes were on fire.

"Father, what happened?" Stuart asked.

"Gabe!" Mrs. Franklin cried. "I'm so glad you're here." Scurrying over, she hugged him tight. "What in the world went on down there?"

The doctor spoke slowly, out of breath. "The fire. It spread so fast. Burned the whole row of stores and houses. We only managed to save two. I carried so many buckets of water my arms feel like they'll fall off."

Mrs. Franklin helped her husband to a chair.

"How'd it start?" I asked.

"Nobody knows for sure. The Reverend suspects people were tired of paying high prices for the goods."

"I say let the store burn to the ground," Mrs. Franklin added. "Serves those greedy men right."

"Nobody deserves what happened this morning, Mildred. It was terrible." He ran his fingers through his dirty hair. Black dust fell from his head onto the table, and I knew it wouldn't be any time at all before Mrs. Franklin would have one of us cleaning that up.

"Oh, Gabe, I know it. We hardly have any supplies as it is." Mrs. Franklin wrung her hands. "I didn't mean anybody's house or store should burn to the ground. It's just you were gone so long. I couldn't get Stuart out of bed, I'm worried sick about Molly and Peter, and I had to prepare this meal practically by myself." She babbled on, not letting Dr. Franklin talk anymore about the fire. After she complained for what seemed like hours, she calmed down and rested in her rocking chair.

I helped Olivia clear the dishes and clean up the meal. I noticed she had a small cloth wrapped around her hand, probably to cover the burn from Mrs. Franklin's coffee yesterday. Soot covered her clothes like the doctor's, but she had to keep working just the same. She didn't get to rest. Sometimes I wondered why Olivia didn't just run away. I heard the Franklins talking about the Smiths' slaves and how two of them had run for freedom to the North. The master had caught and whipped one of them so bad that he wouldn't be working for a month. Maybe somebody spilling coffee on your hand was better than risking your life for freedom.

Dr. Franklin interrupted my thoughts. "Did your brother make it back?"

"What do you mean?" I swallowed hard.

"He was downtown, helping out with the blaze." Dr. Franklin leaned on his elbow.

"I thought that's where he went, but I wasn't sure." My hands began to tremble, and I put down the china plate. "Maybe then he went to get my journal."

Mrs. Franklin gasped. We all turned and looked at her, and she dabbed her eyes with her handkerchief.

I grabbed hold of the table. "I told him not to go, but when I woke up this morning, he was—"

"Anna Green," Mrs. Franklin interrupted me once again. "I hope you don't think you're going to be sitting around wasting time writing."

I ignored her and focused on what the doctor was saying.

"James was carrying buckets of water this morning. When I saw him, I told him to get back here immediately because it was no place for him. The fire was burning out of control. He scowled and disappeared, so I figured he had listened."

My head felt light as my knees buckled. I almost fell, except Dr. Franklin sprang up and caught me. Then he helped me sit down. A cold sweat covered my body, wetting the loose hairs at the nape of my neck.

"I'm sure he just went on down and helped with another building." He patted me on the shoulder. "The whole row was burning to the ground. He'll be here soon."

"I need to look for him." I stood and fetched my bonnet from the hat rack.

"We'll send a couple of the servants. You don't need to be out there, too." Dr. Franklin took my bonnet out of my hand and hung it back on the rack.

"He's my brother, and he could be hurt."

"I'll bet my life that he's out messing around. And when he does return, he'll get the whipping of his life." Mrs. Franklin rose from the rocker and went to her room. "Leaving without permission, like a wild Indian, for goodness sake. No manners at all."

"Pa told me Indians aren't wild," I muttered.

Dr. Franklin called to his servants Isaiah and Thomas and whispered to them. They both nodded and set off. An unsettled feeling grew in my stomach and crawled up to my chest. Why wouldn't these people let me take care of my family? Maybe they knew what I knew—I couldn't do it on my own. I watched the two slaves hurry out of the yard until I couldn't see them anymore.

— CHAPTER 13 —
Visitors

"Hello? Anyone home?" a voice called from outside.
I jumped to my feet, hoping it wasn't someone coming to give us bad news about James.

Mrs. Franklin hurried from her room. "Why, Mrs. Lohrs! Sara, Emily! It's so nice to see you. Have you brought us some goodies?" She smiled and revealed her horse teeth.

The Reverend's wife carried a basket. "I brought some things for your family and James and Anna, and a present from an officer the Reverend has befriended. Sara and Emily wanted to help deliver it." She pulled out six yellow June apples, giving three to each of the girls.

It was so wonderful to see Sara, but she didn't look like the happy, little girl we all loved so much. Her eyes drooped, her face was pale, and she was so quiet. She brought my apple first. "Thank you, ma'am," I said and winked at her. She grinned and even giggled a little.

Mrs. Lohrs touched Mrs. Franklin on the shoulder. "My husband said your daughter and grandson were staying at the Balfours'. I wanted to check and see how you are doing."

Still talking in a sweet voice, Mrs. Franklin said, "That's very kind of you." She dabbed her eyes with that lacy handkerchief. "It's very hard."

She tried to put her arm around Sara, but she wiggled loose and came closer to me. I let her take a bite of my apple.

"Anna, I brought you this jar of berry juice and one of the Reverend's old pens," Mrs. Lohrs said. "I know how much you enjoy writing, but the ink's too expensive for us. We've been using this instead for the last few days. The juice works just fine." Her smile filled the room and almost erased my worries.

"That's mighty nice of you, ma'am," I said, even though I didn't have much use for writing now. I needed to concentrate on my family, and how to help them, especially how to keep James from being stupid. No time to write stories or poems in my journal.

"And for James," Mrs. Lohrs said. "Where is he anyway?"

Before I could answer, Mrs. Franklin did. "That little rascal risked his life to go and fight the fire this morning."

I couldn't believe her! She acted like she really loved us. I wanted to tell Mrs. Lohrs how awful she was. But Mrs. Franklin was dangerous—she had poured that coffee on Olivia's hand, and Mrs. Lohrs would probably believe a grown-up over me anyway. Besides, she didn't want us. And it was probably better for Sara to live with the Lohrses, even though I hated it.

"My goodness," Mrs. Lohrs said and gave me an old checkers game for James. "I hope he's all right." As if her words were a signal to the Yankees, the cannons started up again and caused a jar of molasses to splash into a bucket of water below the shelf. "My goodness," Mrs. Lohrs repeated.

I set the game, berry juice, and pen on the table and paced back and forth. My heart beat so hard I thought everyone could hear it over the shelling. I tried not to think of Isaiah and Thomas out there searching for James.

"Where's mine?" Stuart demanded as he walked right up to Mrs. Lohrs with his hand out.

"Stuart, I could never forget you." She reached into her basket and produced a Bible. He frowned, and I covered my mouth to hide a smile. He handed it to his father and went back to his room. Her final gift was sassafras Dr. Franklin could use for tea.

Mrs. Lohrs asked again when James left this morning, and the doctor stepped outside to see if he was coming. The women discussed the fire, Baby Peter, and how much longer Vicksburg could hold out.

My stomach flipped and twisted. James could be lying in the street, hit by a shell, waiting for us to rescue him. No one was going to stop me from searching for him. I couldn't stand around any longer. I reached for my bonnet.

And that's when he finally returned, unharmed, whistling, and dirty from the fire with, of course, my journal in his hand. I'd never been happier to see anyone in my life. I started to run and hug him, but then I stopped and just stared at him for making me worry so much.

Dr. Franklin spoke first. "You did a very foolish thing this morning, son."

"What?" James waved my journal at him. "I just went to get Anna's journal."

"That's not why you left. You went to help with the fire." The doctor rubbed his hands together. "It was very brave of you, but that fire was out of control, and the bombing was horrible earlier this morning. We were very worried. We want to keep you around for a while—so you can see your pa and brother come home."

Mrs. Franklin interrupted. "I was beside myself." She showed her horse teeth to Mrs. Lohrs again.

"I didn't do nothing wrong," James protested. "Those people needed help, and I heard Reverend Lohrs say he needed all the men down there."

Dr. Franklin was quiet for a few moments. "If you really wanted to help, you should have told someone where you were going."

"She wouldn't have let me go." James pointed at Mrs. Franklin. "She's mean, nasty, and terrible."

I couldn't wait to see what the busybody would do, with James accusing her right in front of the Reverend's wife. Before Mrs. Franklin had a chance to defend herself, her husband ordered James to leave the room. My brother relented, then handed me my journal. "Thank you," I whispered.

"Well, Mildred, I best be on my way," Mrs. Lohrs said. I wanted to run to her, grab her skirt, and not let go until she agreed we could leave with her. But I wouldn't act childish anymore. Too many people depended on me.

"You don't have to go so soon, do you?" Mrs. Franklin said in a high-pitched voice.

"Yes, I'm afraid so. I have a lot of people to see today. They're upset about the stores and homes burning. Wondering where they'll get supplies to cook and feed their families."

A shell landed close and shook the cave. Mrs. Lohrs glanced at Emily and Sara, who held hands in the corner. "Maybe the girls could stay here, until the shelling stops again at suppertime."

Mrs. Franklin looked like she wanted to pass out, but the fake smile reappeared, and she said, "Just take your time. These girls are the sweetest things." Her old horse teeth reappeared, too.

"Are you going to leave now while the Yankees are bombing?" I asked.

"I'm used to it, but I don't want to scare the girls. I'm not going to let Grant's men stop me from doing the Lord's work." She hugged me, then tied her yellow bonnet and went out with a wave of her hand. Dr. Franklin followed, asking if she knew any more about the fires.

As soon as they left, Mrs. Franklin sneered at me and grabbed my journal. I remembered my last entry— the one where I wrote all the mean things about her. I couldn't let her read it!

— CHAPTER 14 —
Dancing Flames

I snatched my journal from Mrs. Franklin and held it against my chest.

"Let me see that, Anna Green! My name was in there."

"No, ma'am." I hugged it tighter.

"Hand it over."

Dr. Franklin walked back into the cave. "What's this?"

"Gabe, she's written about me." Mrs. Franklin reached for the book. "This is my home, and I want to see that book!"

"Mildred," Dr. Franklin said. "It *is* the girl's diary."

She turned her glare from me to bat her eyelashes at her husband. "Please, dear."

"What difference does it make what she says about you?" He lifted the book out of my hand, then shook it in her face. "It doesn't matter." He placed it with authority on the table, left his hand on it while looking at us both, and walked into his room.

Did he really think that would stop Mrs. Franklin from taking my journal? Maybe he was worn out from treating all the wounded. He never had enough supplies, so he couldn't be bothered with his wife and my silly diary. She plopped down in her rocking chair and picked up her knitting, but I kept my eye on her.

Maybe I should have been worrying about more important things like whether or not our citizens were going to have enough to eat next week, or our soldiers would have enough supplies to keep fighting. Or if Pa and Michael had enough strength to fight and still make it home alive.

But I had to show Mrs. Franklin she couldn't push me around. Nobody could. Besides, why did she care so much what my journal said? She seemed awful worried about what I had written. The story Stuart told James about his ma giving food to the Yanks crossed my mind, but I just couldn't believe she would be that dishonest. Anyway, I didn't want her to read it, no matter what I wrote in there. The journal was mine.

I strolled over to the table to pick it up, but I was too slow. Mrs. Franklin was much closer and threw down her knitting, grabbing it first.

"I won't let you read it." I reached for the book, but she moved away.

"Just try and stop me," she whispered and glanced over her shoulder to see if Dr. Franklin was coming.

While she flipped through the pages, I took advantage of her not watching me and snatched the journal. I hurried just outside the cave, wrapping my arms around the book like it was more precious than fresh vegetables.

The cannons' booms echoed through the town. A shell hissed above us. Which was worse—Mrs. Franklin reading what I wrote or a cannonball striking me? I stepped backward and glanced up.

Mrs. Franklin lunged for my journal but grabbed my wrist instead. I switched the book to my other hand. Another bomb raced through the sky. Her fingers inched toward my diary.

"Anna," Sara called. "What are you doing?"

"Go away, Sara."

I looked around for a place to run. There was the oak tree or the house—and neither seemed safe. Then I saw Olivia boiling a pot of water. Her eyes met mine. She looked to the fire and nodded. I knew what she was hinting at. I took a deep breath and ran to the fire. I hesitated just a second, casting my eyes side to side before I flung my journal into the flames.

As the flames gobbled up my stories, I fought to keep my hands from reaching in and saving the poem about how rotten James was or my story about the old man and his foolish children or even my feelings when Pa and Michael left to join the army.

"Well, we won't have to worry about you wasting your time writing now, will we?" Mrs. Franklin whispered in my ear. "You're a strange girl."

The flames danced around my journal; the pages crackled and disappeared, and I was convinced I would never write another word. I had nothing left to say.

"You better not stand there all day. Shells are flying over," Mrs. Franklin called as she made her way into the cave.

Olivia took my hand, and I felt the bandage on hers. Anger boiled inside of me so much so I might have been the one exploding soon instead of the bombs. How could all this have gone wrong in such a little time, just because the Yankees decided to take over Vicksburg? It wasn't fair. And I couldn't seem to do anything but make things worse for James, Sara, and me.

Olivia let go and stirred the pot again. Watching her, I understood why some of the slaves wanted to be on their own, with people like Mrs. Franklin around controlling their lives.

"Anna?" Sara's voice startled me. "Come back inside."

I took her hand and squeezed. "You go inside with Emily. There's nothing to worry about out here. I'll be there in a minute."

"Where's your diary?" She looked up at me, eyes wide. "Does she have it?" Her blonde braids glistened in the sunlight.

"No, I burnt it," I whispered.

"You did? What for?"

"Quit asking so many questions." I let go of her hand and gazed at the fire. "I wasn't planning on writing anyway. I've got too much work to do."

She clutched my hand.

"Go inside." I let go and tried to push her along before another shell sailed through the clouds. The flames crackled with delight like they were destroying not only my words but my hopes and dreams, too.

"I don't want to," she said. "I want to be with you." Sara winced and tugged at my arm when a shell flew over. It exploded next to the large apple tree in the Franklins' yard, shaking the ground like the earth was splitting in two. Tiny apples fell onto the grass.

"Get yourselves inside," Olivia yelled. "The bombs is landing closer." Her words seemed to put a target on the Franklins' yard. Another cannonball flew over our heads and crashed through the roof of their house.

Boom! One more shot rang from the cannon. The three of us darted inside just as another bomb fell from the sky like a shooting star. The explosion knocked me down onto my stomach. Had I been hit? Is this what Ma felt like when she died? I felt my back and hips and patted both my legs with my arms, then felt my stomach. My hands felt fine—nothing sticky, no blood.

The roar pierced my ears. Smoke swept into the cave. While I lay there, my eyes watered so much I couldn't see Sara or Olivia. Panic swept over me, causing every inch of my body to feel sick, and I gagged to keep my dinner down.

"Sara," I tried to choke out.

With my lungs full of smoke, all I could do was cough. I crawled on the floor and patted it with my hands, frantically searching for Sara. I wouldn't allow myself to think the worst.

My fingers raced along the floor until they hit her small foot. My fingertips followed her knee, not pushing too hard in case something had broken. When I reached her stomach and felt her ribs move up and down, I knew she was breathing.

Then I heard Olivia praying, "Let those children be safe."

"Girls, are you all right?" Dr. Franklin's voice rang through the pain in my head.

"Yes sir," I managed to say. "But I don't know about Sara."

He waved his arms through the smoke and coughed as he lifted her into his arms. I could finally hear her screaming. "Anna, do you need help?" he asked.

"No, I think I can get up," I whispered.

Taking a deep breath, I rolled over on my back and sat up. I rubbed my eyes and saw Olivia stand. She offered a hand and helped me. Limping, I followed Dr. Franklin and Sara into our room where James sat on the quilt with his arms crossed, upset about something. I figured Dr. Franklin ordered him to stay put. Emily played safely in the corner with Betty the doll.

"What happened?" He ran over to the doctor and took Sara from him.

She sobbed uncontrollably as James lowered her onto the quilt. Her arm had a few small cuts, and a gash bled above her knee. My injuries were about the same.

"I'm not sure what went on out there, son," Dr. Franklin said. "A shell must have hit close to the cave, and the girls were running in." He looked over Sara's cuts, whispering to her and making funny faces. She didn't laugh, but he calmed her down a bit. Then, he took my arm and felt the bones. "Nothing seems broken. Are you in a lot of pain anywhere?"

My stomach hurt from landing on it, and I figured I'd have some bruises. But nothing on my body felt any worse than the time I tripped and fell into a rose bush when I was Sara's age. It took forever for Ma to get the thorns out, and I screamed for hours. Michael laughed and laughed and called me Miss Anna Thorn for a week. I didn't find that too funny. "I think I'm fine. Thank you, Dr. Franklin."

"Then I'll get some water to wash your cuts."

"Why were you out there?" James picked a ball off the floor when the doctor left.

Sara took a deep breath and wiped her eyes. "Mrs. Franklin tried to get Anna's journal. And she put it in the fire." She took Betty after Emily offered the doll to her.

"You mean the journal I went to get?" James threw his ball against the dirt wall, and it landed with a thud.

"I didn't ask you to," I reminded him.

"The whole reason I'm in trouble with them . . . ," he pointed into the rest of the cave, "is for your stupid journal." He hollered so loud the neighbors probably heard him over the Yankees' cannons. He stood close to me; our noses almost touched. "And you just threw it away?"

"Yes." I crossed my arms. Besides, the whole reason he was in trouble was because he left to fight the fire without asking permission.

Dr. Franklin entered with a bucket of water and a cloth. He sat down and washed Sara's legs and arms, but I didn't take my eyes off James. "Anna," Dr. Franklin said.

I turned my head slightly to show respect. "Make sure to clean your cuts thoroughly."

"Yes, sir." I stared at my brother as the doctor left the room. I had expected him to say something about getting into an argument at a time like this, but he probably understood I had to take care of James. If my brother wanted a fight, I was ready for a battle. James was nothing compared to what I'd just been through.

He must have sensed I would whip him because he said nothing else about my diary. He backed away, whistled, and picked up his ball again. He threw it into the air. "We should go home."

"No," I said just to be argumentative. I wanted to get away from Mrs. Franklin, too. I wanted to show Pa that I was capable of taking care of this family. I wanted Ma to look down from Heaven and be proud of me.

"Why not?"

"Because we would starve." I dipped the cloth into the water and tended to my cuts. I would tell him later that I was considering it.

James put the ball down and sat on the quilt next to Sara and Emily, who had her arm around my sister. "George and Noah got food. They'd share with us."

I rinsed the cloth in the bucket and then took extra care with the cut on my elbow. It stung awful. If this little cut hurt so badly, I bet our soldiers screamed in pain when a bullet tore their skin open. Sara and I were lucky.

James was right about George and Noah, but the only thing holding me back, the only thing I really worried about was James's and Sara's safety. Ma had died when I was with her. Sara and James could, also.

"And plus—"

Mrs. Franklin's voice boomed from the other room, interrupting James. "We have to sign it. Please, Gabe, please."

— Chapter 15 —
The Petition

"What's she talking about?" my brother whispered.

"I don't know." I saw Reverend Lohrs in the next room. "Let's go see."

James helped Sara and Emily up, and we went to get a closer look. Reverend Lohrs held a piece of paper with some writing on it. Dr. and Mrs. Franklin faced each other with their hands on their hips like James and I had a few minutes ago. Seemed like we were all busy battling each other instead of the Yanks.

"Mildred, I'm not putting my name on that document. It shows weakness." He turned away. "Thank you, Reverend, for coming by and letting us know about the petition, but we don't want any part in signing it."

"Petition? What's that?" Stuart entered the room. He carried a small piece of metal behind his back.

"Well, son," Dr. Franklin said. "Some people in Vicksburg want our general to tell Grant's army to stop firing at the city long enough to allow the citizens to leave. If enough people sign it, that might happen."

"Oh," Stuart answered.

I could tell he didn't understand what his father had said. But I did. Leave the city? Where would we go? Michael would never find us, then. Maybe Pa neither.

"Excuse me, Reverend Lohrs," I said. "How many names do you have on that petition?"

"Two so far." He smiled at me and raised his bushy eyebrows.

Mrs. Franklin paced back and forth, fanning herself. "Gabe, we must sign it. I'm hungry all the time and tired of living like some underground rat!"

Dr. Franklin stepped in front of his wife and took her hand. "Answer me this, dear, where will we go? Grant has destroyed everything around us. We have no food supply for a trip. We'll be as safe here as anywhere. The Yankees will never overtake Vicksburg."

I wanted to agree with him but knew to keep quiet.

"He's probably right, Mildred," Reverend Lohrs said.

The two men huddled with her until she announced she needed to lie down for a while. Her husband took her into the other room and left us alone with the Reverend.

"The doctor mentioned you had a scare today. I'm glad to see you girls are fine." He playfully flipped Sara's braid, but she just looked down.

"Yes, sir." I flipped Sara's other braid, and she finally giggled.

"How are y'all holding up here?"

James answered before I could. "We hate it and want to go home, but Anna won't take us."

Reverend Lohrs glanced at me, and my brother spoke again before I had a chance to say anything.

"Mrs. Franklin's mean, and we're going hungry. We barely get anything to eat."

I glared at him, but he ignored me.

The Reverend rubbed his forehead. "Everyone's hungry, son. Help's coming. I'm sure of it." He looked directly at James. "Just be patient. I'll see if I can find out any more about Michael."

Dr. Franklin returned and invited Reverend Lohrs to sit at the table. While Olivia poured them some coffee—probably hickory instead of acorn—they discussed something quietly. I strained to hear their voices over the noise outside. James walked to the cave's entrance and looked out at the sky. I tapped him on the shoulder, motioning for him to come away, but he ignored me.

"I must keep circulating this petition." Reverend Lohrs took a big drink from his cup and made a face, then stood and pushed in his chair. "God be with you and keep you safe." He put on his hat and was gone.

I hoped he wouldn't find any more people to sign that paper. If he did, maybe I could start my own petition. A petition that said some of us wanted to stay right here, in the caves, and protect our city. If we left, I bet the Yankees would come in and take our belongings. They would live in our houses—they wouldn't have to stay in the caves because no shells would be flying over anymore. Dr. Franklin was right. We shouldn't let the Blue Bellies drive us from our city.

I wouldn't leave. When General Lee wrote me back, he wouldn't know where to send the letter if I was living in the country somewhere. I planned what my petition would say and how I could go around getting signatures without putting myself in danger. I had to stay safe for James and Sara. Plus, Mrs. Franklin would probably tear it up if she found it. Obviously, she didn't want to stay here.

"Anna." Dr. Franklin awoke me from my planning. "Sara and Emily need to go back home now. It's supper time, and the skies are quiet."

I didn't want Sara to go. After what happened with the explosion earlier, I couldn't stand the thought of her leaving. I wanted to take care of my sister myself. She needed to be with me. I could protect her just as well as the Lohrses could—even from Mrs. Franklin.

"Dr. Franklin, I want Sara to stay here."

He shook his head. "I just don't think that's possible. The Lohrses are expecting both of the girls back tonight."

"If we explain to Mrs. Lohrs how Sara and I were almost killed this afternoon, I know she'll let her stay. I don't want to be away from Sara during this."

The doctor ran his fingers through his hair and smiled. "I'm not so worried about Mrs. Lohrs."

"Anna!" Mrs. Franklin shouted from her room. "Come here this instant."

I strolled over to her room.

"Sara will leave with Emily as planned." She lay on her mattress with her head propped on three pillows.

"Calm down, dear. You're working yourself into a panic." Dr. Franklin handed her a glass of water, and she kissed him on the cheek. "Let's have a calm discussion about this, Mildred. There's been quite enough excitement for one day."

An idea formed in my mind as I watched her fan herself. Mrs. Franklin couldn't force me to cover up the truth any longer. It was risky if I told the truth about what I'd seen here, but it was my only hope.

"Dr. Franklin, I need to tell you something about Olivia and the bandage on her hand." I looked right at his wife, who reminded me of a hog basking in the sun.

"What is it?" he asked.

"Well," I paused, giving Mrs. Franklin the opportunity to stop me. "I know how she burned herself. She wasn't careless."

"No?"

"No, sir."

"You see," I waited again and stared at Mrs. Franklin.

She tried to prop herself up on her elbows, but fell back down. "Yes, Gabe, I meant to tell you myself. You see, I accidentally spilled some coffee on Olivia's hand the other day. I felt so horrible about it that I asked her to keep it a secret. I didn't want to have to think about it again."

Dr. Franklin rubbed his hands together. "That does happen sometimes, dear. But next time, you need to tell me when our slaves are injured. I am the master of this house."

I rolled my eyes and kept thinking about a way to keep Sara here. "And doctor, about my journal the other day."

"Yes?" He raised his eyebrows.

"You see." I talked real slow, glancing at the busybody. "After you went to rest, I—"

"Oh, all right, Anna Green. Sara can stay." Mrs. Franklin managed to prop herself up this time. "But she better not get in the way."

"Yes ma'am." I smiled like it was my birthday.

"Well done." Dr. Franklin clapped his hands one time. I felt warm and tingly inside for the first time since that awful day Ma had been taken from us. I could do this. I could take care of my family. I just needed a little time to work things out, and then we'd be on our own. The ache in my chest lightened while I practically skipped to tell Sara she could stay with James and me.

— CHAPTER 16 —
Albert

I worried and worried we'd have to leave Vicksburg.
The next day before the noon meal, I snuck out of the
cave while Mrs. Franklin helped Stuart clean a cut. Hurrying across the yard with the berry juice Mrs. Lohrs
gave me, I burst in the Franklins' house and found Dr.
Franklin's desk and a sheet of paper. There wasn't much
left, but I needed only one. I grabbed a quill in another
drawer and sat down in the middle of the dust and
broken glass and loose boards to write my petition.
Although I had no idea what a petition should say.

While I dipped the pen in the berry juice, I thought
about Reverend Lohrs's petition and tried to remember the wording.

Citizens of Vicksburg, I wrote, pressing down hard
on the page. The berry juice didn't show up very well,
and I had to trace over my words three times. Pea bread,
acorn coffee, berry juice—these items must show the
Yankees we wouldn't give up easily. Maybe I would get
plenty of signatures on this petition then. No one
wanted to surrender, did they?

I continued writing, retracing my words so they could be read easily. *Please sign your name below if you want to stay in Vicksburg and protect our city from the Yankees. Do not be weak! Do not be scared! We are strong.* Then, I signed my name.

I threw the pen back in the drawer, slammed it shut, and ran out the back. I sprinted across the yard, sweating more from my nerves than the heat and exercise. Just before I got to the cave's entrance, I slowed down, took a deep breath, and walked in with the petition and berry juice behind my back.

"Be quiet. This is going to make it feel better," I heard Mrs. Franklin say to Stuart from the other room, and I knew they were still tending to his cut.

James and Sara waited for me at the table. "Did you do it?" James asked.

"It's right here." I waved the paper in the air.

Sara brushed Betty's hair with my hairbrush. "When are people gonna sign it?"

I had decided to hide the petition in our trunk until I needed it. If I heard word that Reverend Lohrs got enough signatures, I would start circulating my petition right away. No use causing trouble or risking my life if I didn't need to. "In a couple of days," I said while I buried the petition under some clothing in our trunk.

More and more, I kept thinking that maybe I should take Sara and James home. George and Noah were good servants, so the cave they built for us could probably withstand anything the Yankees shot at it. I bet it was one of the safest places in Vicksburg. If we moved there, then we would be free to do whatever we needed to do to stay together, to find Michael, and to remain in Vicksburg. And somehow I'd figure out a way to help Olivia.

I could do several chores on my own now, and I bet Mrs. Lohrs would help us with the sewing if we needed. Ma had taught her well. After Ma gave her those lessons, Mrs. Lohrs sewed us the most beautiful quilt with dark red and navy blue patterns. Ma had put it right on her bed because she was so proud. Pa said, "We need to have a celebration because your ma is such a grand teacher."

Pa never missed a chance to have a party. Nellie had made ham and beans and cherry cobbler with ice cream while Ma sat in a rocker and soaked her feet in a tub of warm water. A longing started in the bottom of my stomach and rose to my chest and my throat. I closed my eyes tight to see Ma with her feet in the tub while Pa stood above her rubbing her shoulders.

Mrs. Franklin bustled out, wiping her forehead with a handkerchief. "That boy," she whispered under her breath before she saw us sitting at the table lost in our thoughts.

"Nothing to do, children?" she asked. "Is dinner prepared?"

"What dinner?" I looked out the cave to see if Olivia was cooking anything on the fire. I didn't want her to be in trouble again. "I mean, ma'am, there isn't much food to go around. Maybe a piece of ham and tiny cup of milk for each of us. Olivia's still working on the pea bread."

"I can't take any more of this." Mrs. Franklin fell into her rocking chair as the cannons started up again.

One shell after another flew above us and exploded somewhere, maybe killing grass or farm animals or even someone's ma. Sara flinched each time the cannons sounded until she finally laid her head on the table.

"Where's the doctor?" Mrs. Franklin looked like she would faint. "He was supposed to be back for his meal."

"Here I am, dear." He rushed in and went to his wife, kissing her on the cheek. In his hand, he carried a narrow strip of wallpaper, torn around the edges.

"What do you have there?" Mrs. Franklin rocked back and forth.

"It's *The Daily Citizen*."

Stuart came out of his room with a large bandage wrapped around his elbow. "That ain't the newspaper." He crossed the room to get a better look.

Dr. Franklin showed both sides to his son. "The editor has run out of paper. He's determined to get the news out, so he's using wallpaper."

"What does it say?" Mrs. Franklin fanned herself so profusely that the exercise probably made her sweat more.

"Great news, my dear! General Johnston is coming. He should be here in no time to take back our city from the Yanks."

"Amen."

Stuart took the pale yellow paper from his pa. He flipped it over and over, not even trying to read the words. Mrs. Franklin placed her hand out for Stuart to hand it to her, and he did. She held it near a candle and squinted at the print. More than anything, I wanted to grab it from her and read it myself, but I didn't feel like arguing. I felt so hungry and didn't have energy to do anything else after writing the petition.

But if Johnston was coming soon, maybe I could take Sara and James home now. We wouldn't be on our own very long before this shelling stopped, and our troops brought us some food.

"Johnston is my hero!" Mrs. Franklin tossed down the paper.

"I'm so hungry, Mother," Stuart whined. "It's like I ain't even eaten."

"We're all hungry." Dr. Franklin picked up the paper again. "But we'll make it. According to this, we'll be back to normal and out of this cave in less than a week."

"That's too long," Stuart complained.

While I daydreamed about telling Mrs. Franklin I was taking James and Sara home, someone rushed in out of breath.

"Aunt Mildred! Uncle Gabe!" He doubled over and grabbed his side.

I was surprised their nephew, Albert, was visiting now, but I was glad to see him. The bombs flew overhead as heavy as the day Ma was killed. But at least they weren't landing too close to the cave.

"What's the matter, Albert?" Dr. Franklin asked.

"Our cave. It's fallen in and killed a servant." He stopped to catch his breath.

"Is my sister hurt? Where are the twins? What happened?" Mrs. Franklin hurried over and pulled a chair out for him to sit down.

"All of us but our servant, Billy, managed to get out when the first shell exploded. He was in the other room when the roof collapsed. His pa and some of the other Negroes dug him out, but it was too late." Albert dropped into the chair. Smudges of dirt covered his tanned face and mixed with sweat pouring off his forehead. Sara stared at him wide-eyed, and I gently swatted her hand to break her trance.

"Where's my sister?" Mrs. Franklin cried.

"The rest of us ran down to the cellar."

"They aren't safe there." Dr. Franklin took his hat from the rack.

Olivia brought Albert a cup of water. He drank it slowly before he spoke again. "That's why Mother sent me here. We want to stay with you."

"No!" Stuart shouted. I imagined he was thinking about Albert's twin sisters, Penelope and Nellie. They were nine years old and a little prissy. "There are too many people in here already taking my food."

"Stuart, hush up." Dr. Franklin turned to Albert. "Son, of course you can stay. I'll go with you to gather your family and bring them here."

James had to open his big mouth. "What makes this cave any safer than theirs? They should stay at home."

James would be pestering me more than ever to go back to our cave now, and before Albert came running in, I was ready to tell him yes. But if caves were collapsing and killing people, I'd rather stay where more people could help us dig somebody out. I wished General Johnston would come tonight. Then everyone could live in their houses again, and we wouldn't have to give in to the Yankees. We'd have food, and our boats would be able to travel up and down the Mississippi.

Dr. Franklin answered James patiently. "Our cave's very secure. I'm sure you've noticed the boards across the ceiling." We all looked up. "Why, we've hardly had crumbs of dirt fall."

I looked around at the furniture. If the roof was so secure, then why did a layer of dust cover everything? Why did I have to wash the table and chairs every day? Why did I pick dirt out of my hair every morning?

James stormed into the other room when Albert and Dr. Franklin left. Having four more people in this cave would be hard, especially with the twins. Hopefully, they'd bring food to share, and I *would* get to see Albert all the time.

After his pa died, Albert's family had moved here from New Orleans. I fancied him since the first time I saw him at church, especially because he was two years older and taller than me. All the boys my age hadn't caught up to my height yet.

I felt awful sorry for Albert and couldn't imagine waiting to see if George could dig Noah out of a collapsed cave. Sometimes, Noah seemed almost like our brother.

Oh, Albert. His large, brown eyes seemed so sad. I remembered when Ma had noticed how much I liked him. It was at the church social last summer. While I was eating the biggest piece of watermelon ever and a gallon of juice was running down my chin, Albert came over to say hello. I turned as pink as the watermelon and muttered a hello back.

When he left, Ma put her arm around me and whispered, "He is quite handsome with his lightly freckled cheeks. Looks a little like your father did when he was that age. And he looks at you like your father used to look at me."

I smiled at her with my stomach twisting in knots at how silly I must have seemed to him.

How would I ever make it living in the same cave with him?

— CHAPTER 17 —

Buzzing Bees

When Albert's family arrived after suppertime, the Franklins busied themselves in Molly's old room. They rearranged mattresses, so Albert and Mrs. Whitcock would have a comfortable place to sleep. The cannons were quiet, and it seemed as if the Yankees had taken a break for the night.

"I ain't sharing my bed with nobody." Stuart crossed his arms.

"Anna, get the girls' belongings and move them in with y'all," Mrs. Franklin ordered. "You make them feel right at home." She handed me so many quilts I couldn't see over them.

Nellie and Penelope watched me carry their trunks and bedding. At least James helped, so I didn't have to do it alone.

In our room, I put down a pallet for the twins and covered it with blankets. The five of us sleeping in there would be a tight fit.

The twins strolled into the room once the work was done. They were the exact opposite of Sara with dark, straight hair fixed in tight braids. At the end of each braid, their mother tied a perfect pink bow that matched their frilly, lacy pink dresses. Looking at them, no one would have known we were in the middle of a war.

"We haven't got enough room in here." Penelope fussed with her bedding, spreading it out even more.

"We'll surely be squished," Nellie complained.

The girls pushed our quilt into the corner. Now only one person could fit on it instead of the three of us.

"Don't you two prissy girls come in here and try to take over." James kicked their bedding to the side and spread out our quilt. "We were here first."

"James, hush up." I evened everyone's bedding, so we would all have equal room.

"I like your hair bows," Sara said quietly.

Penelope looked at my sister's hair and said, "Maybe you could borrow Nellie's bows one day." A tattered blue ribbon held Sara's curls—the same ribbon she had worn the day Ma died.

"She can't borrow my ribbons," Nellie whined to her sister. "She should borrow yours. Yours are better."

Sara looked down and didn't say anything. But not James. He could never keep his mouth shut. "It wouldn't matter what you had in your stinkin' hair. It's ugly all the same."

"If you aren't nicer to us, I'll tell Aunt Mildred. She'll throw you out." Penelope stuck out her tongue.

"Good." James crossed his arms. The twins turned their back on him and untwisted their hair for bed.

"Really, it shouldn't be too hard for us to get along," I said, keeping the peace like Ma used to do with James and me. "There are so many awful things going on in Vicksburg. We shouldn't be mean to each other, too."

The girls faced me with guilty looks. They both mumbled, "Sorry."

"Did you hear the girls?" I turned to James. "They said they were sorry."

James said nothing, but Sara replied, "That's all right."

I spoke for James since he refused to even look at us. "Nellie and Penelope, James is sorry, too."

He gave me a dirty look.

Sara sat on the floor in front of the twins' pallet while Penelope brushed my sister's curly blonde hair. The night was hot and sticky. I went into the other room to get a cup of water and to hopefully see Albert before I went to sleep. He was playing his guitar in the candlelight.

"Hello, Anna," he said quietly.

My stomach felt like a swarm of bees buzzed inside it. "Hello."

"Are my sisters giving you problems yet?"

I didn't want to complain, and they really weren't that bad. "Not at all."

He strummed a few chords. "Just wait. It won't take them long to get over what happened tonight. They'll be back causing trouble before you know it." His face lit up like the morning sky.

"Kind of like James."

He laughed, then his face got serious. "Uncle Gabe said you haven't heard from Michael or your pa yet. I'm awful sorry."

"Thank you," was all I could manage.

I blinked back tears as I listened to him sing. Sitting across from him, I watched his fingers glide over the strings, and it reminded me of Ma's graceful hands—the way they kneaded dough or braided Sara's hair or sewed a button. Albert's sandy brown hair hung over his forehead and in his eyes. I longed to brush it back for him.

After a while, he stopped and said, "I just read *Oliver Twist*. Have you read it?"

I shook my head no because I couldn't find the words to answer him.

"I remember your pa came to call on us when we first moved to town. He saw the books Mother had and talked about his daughter who loved to read. The books were my father's. He loved reading, too." He glanced down when he mentioned his pa.

I was tired of all this sadness and missed my own pa reading to me more than I could even express. Instead of telling Albert how I felt, how I wondered if I'd ever see Pa again, I said, "I'm awful busy helping out, doing chores," I said. "Not much time for books now."

"Maybe when Johnston comes and life gets back to the way it used to be, you'll have time."

I wondered why everyone thought General Johnston would bring life back to normal. Life for me would never be the same. For all I knew, Pa and Michael might be dead. No matter how great of a general Johnston was, he couldn't bring Ma back. I would always have to live without her. What would normal life be for me? Raising Sara and James by myself while every day we waited to hear if the rest of our family were alive?

"Maybe," I said to Albert, so I didn't trouble him with what I was thinking. And then I didn't know what else to say. Whenever I was close to him, it was like I'd never learned to talk.

He started singing again. I nodded good night to him and turned to leave. He stopped suddenly in the middle of the song and said, "Good evening."

A voice I didn't recognize said the same. I turned around to see who it was. A man a little older than Michael, dressed in dripping wet clothes, stood in front of Albert. He held a letter in his hand.

— CHAPTER 18 —
The Letter

Albert asked the courier to come in. A shell whirred overhead and landed in the Franklins' yard. It shook the cave, along with everything in it. A candle fell over, and Albert rushed to blow it out. At the same time, I put my hands over my ears, lost my balance, and bumped into him. My face flushed, but I had other things to worry about besides being clumsy around Albert. I wanted that letter the courier held. It had to be from Michael.

I pictured Michael arriving in a few days. I smiled thinking of us together again. The courier returned my smile. His red hair clung to his forehead, dripping water onto a skinny nose. A huge cloth bag hung around his shoulder, but it wasn't wet. He must have held it above the water while he swam. I imagined the awful trip he made through the river to bring me my good news.

"Evenin'," the courier said to me and removed his cap.

Albert said, "Shelling is heavy tonight."

"Sure is." The courier stooped over a little. His long skinny legs made him too tall to fit in this cave.

I wanted to snatch that letter out of his hand. When would he give it to me?

Mrs. Franklin bustled into the room, followed closely by Dr. Franklin and Stuart. She greeted him with a stern look. "Young man, you're dripping water everywhere."

"What does that matter?" James hurried into the room. "We're living in a cave."

Mrs. Franklin ignored my brother. Thank goodness. I was tired of listening to the two of them fuss.

"Hello, Robert. Have you got something for one of us?" Dr. Franklin asked.

I could hardly wait to rip it open.

"Yes I do. It's addressed to. . ."

Stuart grabbed it from the courier. He didn't even look at the envelope and started shouting, "To me! To me!" He held it above his head and ran around the cave.

"Stuart, stop this instant." Mrs. Franklin tried to get the letter as he passed.

When he ran by James, my brother stuck his foot out. Stuart fell face first onto the floor.

"He tripped me!" Stuart cried.

"I did not." James crossed his arms.

While Stuart bawled on the ground, I snatched the letter from him and went to a candle. I flipped the envelope over. My stomach sank when I saw who it was addressed to.

"What's wrong?" James came over to me.

"Nothing." I forced a grin. "This is for Molly, from her husband. She'll be so pleased."

"Thank the Lord." Mrs. Franklin sighed. "She's been through enough already. We must get that letter to her first thing in the morning."

"I'll be leaving now." The courier tipped his hat. "Good night, folks."

"Wait." I ran to him. "Dr. Franklin, may I have permission to speak to the courier alone? I have another letter for my brother."

"I don't know, Gabe. Is that appropriate?" Mrs. Franklin held her hand out to Stuart, who was still on the floor.

The doctor winked. "It's fine, Anna."

I rummaged around in the trunk. I didn't have another letter for Michael, but I did have the petition. I grabbed it and held it close to me as I walked outside the cave.

"Ma'am?" The courier removed his hat.

"Do you know Michael Green? Have you seen him or given him any letters lately? Has he been wounded?"

"Whoa there, one question at a time." He put his hat back on. "I had a letter from Reverend Lohrs for him but never did get it delivered. Couldn't find him with the troops."

Tears welled in my eyes.

"But," he continued. "I also haven't heard anything's happened to him. Keep the faith—that's all we can do."

"That's not all we can do. It can't be." My voice rose and almost squeaked like Sara's.

"Robert." Dr. Franklin stepped outside. "Everything all right?"

"Yes, sir."

I turned to the doctor. "Just one more minute, please."

He sighed, rubbed his fingers through his hair, and went back inside.

I pushed the petition in the courier's hand. "Please take this around Vicksburg and ask people to sign it." I didn't know why it was so important for him to do it now, since I hadn't heard any more about the Reverend's petition, but I had to do something for my family.

His eyes scanned the page, and a grin broke across his face. "I'd be happy to, little lady. Anything to save our city from those blasted Blue Bellies."

"Good night, Robert." Dr. Franklin stepped out again, and I knew that was my cue to get inside.

I sat at the table with James and Albert, still thinking about my petition. It was the least I could do for my family and my city. I might not be able to shoot a gun or a cannon, but I could be strong and smart and fight the Yankees in my own way. Our soldiers needed their families to keep life as normal as possible while they fought for us.

The doctor came in and joined us at the table. "Tomorrow, I'll take the letter to Molly along with the baby blanket you made, dear," he said. "It'll be nice to see some happiness. I've witnessed some horrible things at the Balfour house."

"Like what?" Albert held his guitar but wasn't playing it.

"I didn't want to concern you with this before, but, well, these men need their stories told." He looked at me, and I wondered if he expected me to take notes with that berry juice. I stared back at him and waited for him to continue.

"There were some soldiers waiting for the surgeon to cut off their legs and—"

"Why do they have to do that?" Stuart interrupted.

"To stop infection from spreading through the whole body. That would kill them." He lightly tapped his fingers on the table.

James leaned closer to Dr. Franklin. "It would?"

"Yes, James. That's the reason many soldiers lose their limbs."

Mrs. Franklin fluttered around the room. "Gabe, I don't want to hear such nonsense. It makes my stomach sick."

"Mildred, I won't go into detail, but I think it's important the children know how brave our men are, how hard they're suffering for our city." Dr. Franklin stood now and paced back and forth.

"I want to hear." James leaned on his elbows.

"As I was saying." He glanced at Mrs. Franklin. "The soldiers were waiting in the hall, listening to the moans and screams of the men who were already having their limbs amputated. One boy might have only been a year older than you, Anna."

All eyes turned to me.

"Suddenly, a bomb fell through the roof, exploding right on those men who waited for the doctor. It was a terrible scene, one I hope I never witness again."

What if Michael was there, and none of us knew it? What if he was hit with that bomb? Surely if Dr. Franklin had seen him, he would have told me.

Another shell screeched above and exploded closer to us than the last one. The smell of burning grass drifted into the cave, and Albert looked up. Probably to make sure the ceiling wasn't falling in. If he was just a couple years older, he would be expected to sign up with the army, too. I was sure glad he didn't have to fight like Michael.

"I think it's time James and I went to bed." I pushed the words past the lump in my throat.

Once on our quilt, I wished for sleep. But it didn't come. I kept seeing Michael's face.

James rolled toward me. "I thought that letter was from Michael. Maybe even Pa."

"Me too," I answered.

"Maybe they sent a letter to our home," James said.

"Shhh," I whispered. "You don't want to wake up Sara and the twins."

He jerked away from me. If he only knew how close I'd been to taking us home.

Early in the morning, I left my siblings and the twins asleep and went into the other room where Mrs. Franklin stood at the back entrance, waving her handkerchief and calling, "Not 'til Wednesday, you hear me?" Then she turned around quickly, patted her mouth with the cloth, and barked an order at Olivia.

I wondered who she was talking to. Was it some Yankee soldiers? Could James and Stuart be right? Maybe I should let James solve this mystery. I didn't want to live with a traitor. Mrs. Franklin hates the Yanks, though. I looked up and saw her staring at me. She gave me her usual glare.

"Did Dr. Franklin leave to see Molly already?" I tied an apron around my waist.

"No," Mrs. Franklin said. "Mrs. Thomas is having her baby, and the poor thing is suffering so. Dr. Franklin took Albert to help."

"Oh." My stomach sank a bit. I wouldn't see Albert this morning.

"We've got three more mouths to feed now. You go help Olivia with breakfast." She plopped down in the rocking chair. "Although I don't see why it really matters. There's hardly any food."

Is that because you're giving it to the Yanks? I wanted to ask her.

While I helped Olivia set the table, I thought about poor Molly and how she needed that letter. She'd always been kind to me. And if Michael was at the Balfours', I'd have a chance to look for him. Maybe there were so many wounded, Dr. Franklin hadn't been able to see my brother.

"Mrs. Franklin," I said.

"What?" she snapped.

"I'll take the letter to Molly."

"You have too much to do around here."

I turned my back and counted to ten. Something Pa tried to teach James to do, but he wasn't very successful.

"Well," she interrupted when I was on eight. "I guess you'll have to. Heaven knows when Gabe'll be back. And I surely can't trust the Negroes."

I was glad she'd agreed. I'd have time to search for Michael and see for myself what was going on in

Vicksburg. Most people went about their business in spite of the shelling. I didn't see how they did it. Memories of Ma's body flashed in my mind whenever I heard the cannons, making me wonder if any of this would ever end.

— CHAPTER 19 —
Brave Soldiers

When the shelling stopped, I reached for my bonnet. "Mrs. Franklin, I'm going to take Molly's letter now."

"You hurry home. You've got plenty of chores to do," Mrs. Franklin said as I walked out.

Crossing through the Franklins' yard to reach the street, I had to step around craters deep enough that James, Sara, and I could have stood on each other's shoulders and still not reached the top. But some were little enough for a cat to nap in. The holes covered the ground so thick, there was hardly any grass left. I hadn't realized how close some of the explosions had been.

The Balfour house stood above the city like a castle above its kingdom. I was glad to see the shells hadn't damaged it too much. One time before this war, Ma, Sara, and I went to call on Mrs. Balfour when her baby died. Ma sewed a beautiful blanket for her and embroidered "Emma" in pink letters on the corner. Sara and I sat in cushioned chairs while Ma went up the huge staircase to see Mrs. Balfour. That was the only time I had been inside the mansion. I had felt lost in its large rooms with the fancy chandeliers and was glad when we went back to our house with our homemade kitchen table and mismatched curtains.

I wondered if the doctors and nurses ever wished the hospital were in a cave, so they would be better protected. Almost everyone in Vicksburg lived underground. But a cave wasn't big enough to hold an entire hospital, although Mrs. Franklin thought hers was. She would never stand for all that mess inside. Besides, caves were not well lit. It was practically impossible to sew a straight stitch on a pair of pants, let alone perform surgery on a poor soldier.

I climbed the steps and admired the tall brick house with its long windows and balconies without any railings. The army had probably removed them to use the iron for weapons. Shells had cracked and broken some of the beautiful windows, now patched up with boards. The roof had a few holes in it just like all the rest of the houses in town. The Yanks didn't care if people were rich or poor; they shot at everyone just the same.

The door hung open, and I could see people rushing around trying to take care of the men lying on cots in the hallway. One man was trying to reach a canteen on the edge of his bed. I hurried in to help him and covered my nose to keep from gagging. The hallway smelled worse than when my grandfather's dog, Cadet, died. After helping the man drink from his canteen, I went on my way, looking for Molly.

Another soldier moaned and moaned in pain—he had only a bandage where his leg used to be. The doctors probably cut it off to stop infection from spreading through his body and killing him.

"Miss," he spoke barely above a whisper.

"Yes, sir?" I said, although he didn't look much older than me.

"I'm so hot."

A pan of water sat on a piano bench nearby. I knew it wouldn't be cold, but I wet a cloth anyway, and then put it across his forehead. He tried to smile, but his glassy eyes just stared at me. I hurried past, wishing I would find Molly soon.

Black streaks from shells that had found their way into the house splattered one wall, and some of the floorboards were missing. I passed more cots full of men with strips of stained cloth wrapped around their heads, their arms, and their legs. Looking at each one, I searched for Michael, hoping he wouldn't be in this awful place, even though I wanted desperately to find him.

At the end of the hallway, I felt a hand grab my arm. I snapped my head around to see another stranger. I struggled to pull away and noticed the blood-soaked bandage around his waist.

"Please girl, hand me that whiskey." He pointed at my feet where a broken bottle lay.

"I'm sorry, sir," I managed to choke. "The bottle is broken."

"No!" he yelled and tightened his grip. "I'm dying!"

I tried to pull my arm away, but he held it so tight I expected my hand to turn blue. Tears welled in my eyes. Acid rose in my throat, causing me to gag, and the tears to fall down my cheeks. I didn't want to look at him, but when I turned my head, the next bed and the next and all of them had some poor soldier writhing in pain—

men without arms or legs or even eyes that had been poked out and covered with patches.

"Sir, I'm here to help," a voice said. It was Molly! She put a cloth on his forehead.

"Molly, help me." I twisted my wrist, still trying to break free.

"Anna, my goodness, what are you doing here?"

The man continued to moan and hold me. I had to shout over him. "I have something for you."

"Just a minute." Molly pried off his hand and placed a bullet in it instead.

I backed away from them, remembering soldiers bit down on bullets to help with the pain while the doctors operated.

Molly held the soldier's hand and prayed, "Please God, comfort this man in his time of suffering." She wiped the patient's face with a cloth. The man calmed down and quietly moaned.

"Anna, I'm sorry." She turned to me. "What do you have? Something from Mother, I'm sure." She grinned.

"It's a letter from your husband."

Her eyes widened, and she took the letter from me. "Come with me. Let's go outside."

I handed her the baby blanket and followed her through the maze of beds. On the porch, the sun beat down on us, but I was relieved to be away from the men. When she finished reading her letter, I would ask Molly if she'd seen Michael, although she probably would have told me if he was here. I tried to ignore the sinking feeling in my stomach.

While she studied her note, the ache in my chest grew to the size of one of those June apples Mrs.

Lohrs had brought us. I wished that letter were from Michael.

Molly read the words over and over again. "He's safe! Thank God, he's safe." She sobbed and hugged me.

After a few minutes, she wiped her eyes. "Goodness, look at me. I'm a mess. Would you like to see Baby Peter while you're here?"

"I want to." I paused and thought of the story Dr. Franklin told about the bomb exploding on the soldiers. "But I've got to hurry before the cannons start up again."

"Yes, yes, of course." She folded the letter and put it back into the envelope.

"Is Peter feeling better?"

"I don't know." She looked away for a moment, and I knew the answer without her telling me. I searched for the right words, but what do you say to someone whose baby is dying? Just like nobody knew what to say to me when Ma died.

Molly smiled. "Never you mind that. Have you had any word from your family?"

Swallowing hard, I shook my head.

"Something will come soon. I just know it. I never thought I'd get a letter, but I did." She squeezed my hand. "Don't lose hope, Anna. It's all we've got."

I nodded. "Have you seen Michael here anywhere?"

"No, but several soldiers just arrived this morning, and I haven't been around to check them yet." She grabbed my hand. "Let's look a little before we get you home." She led me back into the mansion.

When we reached the back door, a large man blocked our way through the hallway. "You'll have to go around. The doctor's operating."

"Thank you," Molly said.

We entered the ballroom. Dark green paint covered the walls, and long, tattered curtains hung at the sides of the windows—too tired to do their job of blocking the sunlight heating the room. The rows and rows of cots were out of place. Someone had draped sheets over the Balfours' furniture and pushed it into the corner.

I scrunched my nose to cover up the smell as we made our way through. One soldier played a slow, sad melody on his harmonica. I glanced at him and the man next to him. A bandage hid part of the second man's face, but there was no mistaking who he was.

— Chapter 20 —
I'm the One

Michael! I prayed he wasn't dead as I raced to his side. Throwing myself on his chest, I listened for a heartbeat and heard it immediately. He was alive!

"Thank you, God." I stared at his face like it was the first time I'd ever seen him, memorizing every tiny cut on his cheek and chin. His chest rose and fell.

The worst cut he had ran across his chest, above his heart, and was held together with stitches. Was he cut with a knife or barbed wire or a Yankee's sword? Spots of blood stained one of his sleeves. His uniform looked as if a wild dog had taken it in its mouth, shook the shirt and pants as hard as it could, and then ripped at the cloth with its claws.

"Michael," I whispered.

He didn't answer.

"Michael," I spoke louder and leaned over him.

"Anna, I'm sorry." Molly placed her hand on my shoulder. "I didn't know."

"It's all right." I smiled and touched her hand, then went back to waking my brother. I shook his hand a little. "Michael, please. I just want to see your eyes." I scooted a stool over to his cot and sat down, taking his hand again.

The soldier in the next bed quit playing his harmonica. "Brought him in last night." He pointed at Michael. The man, much older than my brother, wore a patch over one eye, and his leg was wrapped to his knee. Dark whiskers covered his chin.

"Was he awake?" I asked.

"No, ma'am. Haven't heard a peep from him." He removed his hat and held out a dirty hand. "My name's Hank, got a bone crushed in this here leg."

Molly took his hand into hers. "Anything I can do for you?"

"I'm doin' just fine." He started playing a tune on his harmonica again. This one I didn't recognize, and I wished he would stop. There was so much noise in the room with the nurses and doctors bustling about and the screaming patients and Hank's whining harmonica. How could my brother sleep through this racket unless something was terribly wrong?

"Why isn't he waking up?" I asked Molly.

"It looks like he suffered a blow to the head." She pointed to the bandage wrapped tightly around his forehead like a lid on a jar. "Sometimes soldiers don't wake up for a while when that happens. Then all of a sudden, they'll sit up in bed and ask for a huge stack of flapjacks or their mama's lemonade."

I studied my brother's face, willing him to wake up. Blood had trickled out from under the wrap and onto his cheek, leaving a dried streak. He breathed in deeply, then pushed out a short puff of air. His face looked peaceful, the way Sara's used to look after Ma rocked her to sleep. Maybe Michael was dreaming of fishing down at the river. That was one of his favorite things to do, except when James tried to tag along.

And then a horrible thought crossed my mind. Since the courier told me he never had the chance to deliver our letter, Michael probably didn't know about Ma. Would I have to tell him that he would never see Ma again? I couldn't do that. He was already suffering so much, I didn't want to rip his insides out, too. I wanted to be the one to help my brother recover—not make him feel worse.

I would have to find someone else to help me. Maybe Reverend Lohrs or Dr. Franklin could break the news to Michael.

"He probably doesn't know about Ma," I whispered to Molly as she handed me a pan full of water and a cloth. "Do you think we could send word to your pa to come here and tell Michael what happened?" I dipped the cloth in water and started to gently wash the cuts on his face.

"Anna, you have—" Molly's voice cracked, and she swallowed hard.

I looked at her, and her eyes shone with tears. She wiped them and said, "You'll have to tell him yourself, when the time is right."

"I won't know when."

"You'll just feel it. When the truth is staring you both in the face, and there's no way around it, you'll tell him in your own way. You can't keep this from him, and there's no better person than you." She adjusted the wool blanket under his arm. "You are in charge of your family now, especially while Michael recovers, and your pa is gone."

I felt more like a little girl than ever before. I was scared, lonely, hungry, tired, and couldn't handle this alone. I sat with him a while longer and watched him sleep, until I just couldn't take it anymore. "Michael." I nudged his arm and spoke his name louder. "Michael."

Wiping dirt off my brother's chin and cheeks, I rubbed carefully between his eyebrows and bandage. "Please, God, let him wake. Not so much for me but for Sara and James." I shut my eyes tight and willed Michael to open his.

I pushed up the sleeves of his uniform and scrubbed his arms, wondering when he last bathed. Ma was always strict on bathing once a week, even in winter. She often had to scold Pa and force him to get into the tub while we stayed in the parlor or in our room. But I loved to listen to Pa when he took a bath because he whistled and sang and belly-laughed. He had so much fun I wondered why Ma always had to force him.

Hank stopped playing and fell asleep. The heat in the room was almost unbearable as the time neared noon. The smell of blood, sickness, and body odor grew worse, along with the flies buzzing around the crystal chandelier. I imagined my brother looking up with his blue eyes and calling me "Squash," his nickname for me. He always said I was squashed up compared to him. I wasn't as tall or strong as him, but I wasn't supposed to be anyway. I hated the nickname, and it made no sense to me. But I'd do anything to hear it now.

Then I felt it—a light squeeze on my hand.

— CHAPTER 21 —

At Last

Michael's eyelashes fluttered like a moth's wings. When they stopped, half-closed, he spoke, "I'm thirsty."

"Michael, you're awake!" I jumped off my stool; it crashed to the floor. "You're awake."

"I'm thirsty."

I could barely hear his words.

"Let me get you some water." I looked around the room for some water that hadn't been used for washing but couldn't see any. I didn't want to leave him to find some. What if he wasn't awake when I returned?

"Molly, Molly!" I shouted and waved my arms frantically through the air. "Michael opened his eyes."

"Quit your hollering," a voice said from a few cots over.

I paid no attention. It wasn't like the room was quiet. "Molly, come quick."

She was removing a bandage from a man's arm and didn't hear me. When our eyes finally met, I said, "Michael needs water," and she hurried over with a canteen.

I tipped it up to him, so a stream could fall into his lips.

"Thanks, Squash," he said before he closed his eyes.

"Try talking to him. It'll help," Molly suggested.

"Michael," I said. "We've missed you."

His eyes fluttered again. "Where am I?"

"You're in the army hospital, at the Balfour house."

"What happened?" He spoke barely above a whisper.

"I don't know. It looks like you were hit in the head. But I think you're going to be just fine."

"It sure does hurt." Michael raised his arm to feel his bandage. "Must have been bad, huh?"

"Yes," I whispered, fighting my tears.

He was silent again, but his eyes didn't close. I searched for something else to say. "Sara and James won't believe I found you."

"Is James being good for Ma?"

He didn't know. He didn't know about Ma. What should I say? "He's behaving all right, I guess. Sara's growing much taller."

"Is she going to pass you, Squash?"

.   I grinned. "Name's Anna. You always seem to forget."

"I got an excuse now." He touched his bandage and tried to smile, but I could tell he felt miserable. "Can I have more water?"

I put the canteen to his mouth. Cannonballs shot through the air, and I wished we were in a cave. I tried not to flinch and look up every time a cannon sounded. A bomb could shatter these glass windows into hundreds of tiny, sharp pieces that might pierce our skin.

The chandelier swayed, and its glass clinked. When a shell exploded close enough, the cots rattled and shook the soldiers in them. Some men screamed; others moaned in pain. It reminded me of the summer when Pa had a broken collarbone. When he rode in our wagon, his body jostled, and he would bite his lip until it bled because his shoulder hurt so badly.

"Have y'all been safe from the Yankees?" Michael let go of my hand to place the lid on the canteen.

"We've been staying in a cave the servants dug out of a hill." I wondered if I should tell him about Ma now. I didn't want to. "What have you been doing?" I asked instead.

"Digging trenches day and night to stop Grant's men. They build tunnel after tunnel, then put dynamite in the holes, trying to blow us away." He shut his eyes tight and scrunched his face.

"Michael! Are you all right?"

Hank woke himself with tossing and turning, probably from a nightmare. He looked over at my brother.

"We've hardly been given any food for the past week," Michael explained. "Only a slice of meat and piece of bread for a day's meal. And that's almost gone now."

"Some fellows are eatin' rats—skinnin' and roastin' 'em over a fire," Hank joined in.

"Rats?" I hoped we wouldn't have to eat those. Then I remembered Mrs. Franklin gossiping about our neighbors and what they were eating. "Some people in town are surviving on meat from their mule."

"Grant thinks he'll starve us into surrenderin'," Hank said. "But we're tougher than those Yanks think."

Michael tried to sit up by supporting himself with his elbows, but he fell back onto the cot. "I feel dizzy."

I wet the cloth and held it to his face, wishing I had some cold water. "I know what'll make me feel better, Squash," he said. "Tell us one of your stories."

"I don't have any you haven't heard." I hadn't written anything since the petition. Stories didn't build up inside me and beg to get out anymore.

"Tell an old one." Michael winked.

"Nothin' better than a good, ol' tale." Hank blew a couple of notes on his harmonica while I fiddled with my braids.

"Most of my stories are for Sara."

"That doesn't matter," Michael said.

I didn't feel like storytelling but did anyway—for Michael. I sat back on my stool and sighed. "There once was a young boy, probably about the same age as James, who was an orphan." I swallowed hard and stopped for a minute, thinking about how James could be an orphan; any of us could be if Pa died.

"He lived with an old woman, Mrs. Butterfield, who had been his parents' neighbor, and she gave him everything he ever wanted, but he wasn't thankful. All he did was sit in his room and play with the toys. He didn't even leave to eat meals with her. She delivered his food to his room."

Embarrassed at my silly story, I stopped and looked at Michael, and he nodded, so I went on and told about how Mrs. Butterfield stopped coming to the boy's room, and how the orphan grew angry and finally came out to investigate.

"Is that it?" Michael rubbed his chin. "Was Mrs. Butterfield dead?"

"Yes, she had a heart attack. I never really finished the story." And the way I felt lately, I probably never would.

"It was real good," Hank said. "I could never make up a tale, but I got one I heard from my sergeant."

Michael glanced at Hank. "Tell us."

"All righty then." Hank put his harmonica down for the first time so he could use both hands to tell the story. "A Yankee soldier lay wounded on the battle-field, callin' out for water. His regiment was gone."

"What happened?" I turned to face him.

"He moaned and begged for help. The only men that heard were his enemy."

"Did he die?" my brother asked.

"Nope, two good ole soldiers from Mississippi climbed out of their trench and carried him to safety, givin' up their own rations for the boy. Why, he was no more than fifteen."

That was the same age as Albert. I was glad he had stayed home to help his ma and sisters. One less person to worry about.

"I need to rest for a while." Michael shut his eyes. "You'll still be here?"

"Yes," I told him.

He fell asleep before another bomb exploded. Hank played his harmonica softly; I barely heard it over the noise in the room. I thought about Mrs. Franklin and how angry she would be when I returned home, but I didn't care. I had stayed the whole day and wouldn't leave now. The Yanks wouldn't quit firing until suppertime, if then.

I kneeled on the floor and laid my head on Michael's cot. The wool from his blanket scratched my face. I pushed the blanket away, cleared a spot, and fell asleep.

When I woke, the courthouse clock rang six times. Michael sat in bed, eating a biscuit. "Are you hungry, Squash?"

My stomach rumbled, but I didn't want to take his food. "No. Just a little thirsty."

He handed me the canteen. I sipped the water, and it tasted like metal. Neither of us said anything. All I could think about was Ma and how he didn't know what had happened to her. I would want to know, and Michael would feel the same. I had already waited the whole day to tell him the news.

"Did you get my letter?" I asked. "Reverend Lohrs sent it with the courier."

"No, sometimes they can't find us." Michael offered me a tiny slice of bacon.

I shook my head. "Michael, the letter I sent was very important, and I'm so sorry you didn't get it." I clenched my fists and took a deep breath. "I have to tell you—"

"What?" he interrupted. He looked at me, and I took another deep breath. "Just tell me, Squash. It'll be all right."

"Ma got hit with a shell."

"She's here? In this hospital? Why didn't you say anything before?"

"No," I cried, swallowing hard and shaking my head.

"She's not here? She's at home?"

I shook my head again. Tears fell from my eyes.

"She died?"

I nodded.

He said nothing, just stared into the room.

"Michael—"

He put his finger to his lips, and a tear slid down his face.

I threw my head down onto his lap, and he gently stroked my hair. We stayed like that for a few minutes before he asked, "Did she suffer?"

"Oh, Michael, no. She fell down, and when James went to her, she had already stopped breathing."

"Thank, God. I've seen so many men die from pain." He took several short breaths like he couldn't get enough air.

I patted his hand while chills ran down my spine at the thought of Ma suffering like that. "She's in Heaven, Michael. She watches over us, and she's still trying to make me into a proper woman, and I still don't always listen to her." I told him about Mrs. Franklin and my plans to take James and Sara home, how Johnston should be here any day, and how George and Noah have hopefully remained in our cave and watched over our house.

"You're right. We'll be fine, Squash." Michael took another sip from the canteen. "What about Pa? Have you heard from him?"

"Yes, a few times, but not lately. The mail takes so long, and the last we heard he was in Virginia." I closed my eyes, wishing I had better news. "But I'm sure he's safe."

Michael tried to smile, but I could tell he was in a lot of pain, and not just from his wounds.

"I wrote a letter to General Lee, explaining how Sara, James, and I needed you and Pa to come home—

maybe y'all could fight here in Vicksburg. That was before I knew you were here for certain. I know it was probably silly, but I was trying anything to get us back together."

"I think it was a fine idea. You never know what Lee will do."

Molly came into the room to light candles on the mantle and windowsills. She walked over to us. "Anna, the bombs have stopped. You should go back to my mother's cave."

"I can't bear to leave Michael." I took his hand and squeezed it.

"I'll be better soon, Squash, I promise. Then I can help you with James and Sara." He let go of my hand. "You listen to Molly. Go on."

I hugged him. "I'm coming back tomorrow, as early as I can."

On the walk home, I had so many feelings inside, like a shell that exploded and broke into a thousand different pieces—so happy to see Michael, so sad to tell him about Ma. Proud of Pa and Michael for fighting against the Yanks, but angry with them for putting themselves in danger. And I had a fight ahead of me with Mrs. Franklin for being gone so long and wanting to go back to the hospital tomorrow. But nothing could stop me from seeing Michael again—not the bombs, not the soldiers, and especially not Mrs. Franklin.

— PART 3 —
On Our Own

— CHAPTER 22 —
A Confrontation

The sky was dark as I made my way back to the Franklins'. Stars twinkled around a skinny moon. Last spring, Pa had shown me how to find the North Star and the Big Dipper. I wanted to sit with him on the front porch like we used to, just hearing stories about this war. I never believed it would touch us.

My eyes watered from the burnt powder in the air. At least that's what I told myself. The cannons were quiet tonight because the Blue Bellies didn't seem to shoot at us when there wasn't much moonlight. I almost skipped as I made my way back to the Franklins'.

When I reached the cave, Olivia and two other slaves were outside picking up debris in the yard. I wondered how they could see, and why the Franklins would have them doing such a job at this time. Inside, Mrs. Franklin and her sister, Mrs. Whitcock, were sewing by candlelight. Mrs. Franklin didn't look up when I came in.

"I found Michael! He's at the Balfour house."

Mrs. Whitcock smiled, but Mrs. Franklin kept stitching.

"He is?" James sprang to his feet, almost knocking over the checkers game he and Albert were playing on the floor.

"Yes, I spent the day with him. He was hurt on the battlefield, but I think he'll be just fine."

Sara rushed into the room. "Will he take us home?"

"I don't know when he'll be able to." I clasped her hand in mine, and we swung our arms back and forth. "But he's going to be well soon," I said. "He can't wait to see you."

"Did he get our letter?" James asked.

"No." I dropped Sara's hand. "I had to tell him about Ma."

James kicked at some dirt with his boot; Sara lowered her head, and I changed the conversation away from Ma's death. I told them all about Hank, his harmonica, and the soldiers eating rats. Mrs. Franklin glared at me during my stories.

"I'm glad you found your brother, Anna." Albert looked up with his huge, brown eyes. "That's good news. We were concerned about you today. I thought maybe Molly convinced you to stay and help her. I'm, I mean, we're glad you're back."

"Thank you." My eyes caught his for a second, and it caused my stomach to flutter even after I looked away.

Mrs. Franklin remained silent and rocked back and forth like a tree's branches in a thunderstorm.

"Did you get to see Molly?" Dr. Franklin shouted over the creaking of his wife's chair.

"Yes, she's well. Do you want me to take something else to her tomorrow?" I paused and whispered my next words to keep Mrs. Franklin from hearing. "I'm going to the Balfour house tomorrow. I promised Michael."

"Well, well, well," Mrs. Franklin said and rose from her chair. She crossed the room and stood so only the table separated us. Her hands rested on her hips like our schoolteacher, whenever she scolded James. "You expect us to believe you were at the hospital all this time?"

"I was, ma'am."

She leaned forward and studied me. "Really?" She wagged her finger. "Wasted your day at the Balfour house?"

I folded my arms and stared right back at her. "Yes, I was helping Michael and some of the others."

"Yes, I know they are very short-handed," Dr. Franklin said without looking up from *The Daily Citizen*.

Sara moved behind me and hid.

"Well, maybe that's true, but I need help around here, too." Mrs. Franklin's voice rang in my ears as if it were a shell falling to the ground.

I bit my lip to keep from bursting into tears. My hands tightened into fists. How could she be so petty? These jobs around here were nothing compared to the work that had to be done at the Balfour house.

I had finally found my brother. And I *would* see him tomorrow. I took a deep breath before I answered, "I can wake early and help out here. Then go see Michael."

She folded her arms across her chest, also. "There's double the work to do here since you were gone all day. I already have my daughter helping those strangers. I don't need you there."

Dr. Franklin finally looked up from his newspaper. "Everyone just calm down. Anna's had a long day, and we can discuss this in the morning when we've all gotten a good night's sleep."

"Thank you, doctor," I said. "I will always do my share while we stay here, but then I'm going to see my brother."

"That sounds like a fine idea, and I'm sure you're a good nurse for Michael." Dr. Franklin stood and placed the paper on the table between Mrs. Franklin and me.

"When did you become the boss of this house?" Mrs. Franklin's glare made me take a step back, and I wasn't sure if she was asking Dr. Franklin or me.

The doctor didn't seem too sure either because he puffed out his chest. "Mildred, that's enough."

"You can't keep us here like slaves!" James interrupted and rushed toward us. He stopped when he reached the table and stood an arm's distance away from Mrs. Franklin.

She took one step toward him and slapped him across the face.

"You mean old witch." I put myself between them. She raised her hand to slap me, but I turned my head. What was wrong with her? I didn't understand how she could be so worried about only herself.

"We're leaving," I announced.

Mrs. Franklin sighed. "That's right, Anna Green. You go on. Go right now if you're so brave." She stepped closer to me, and I turned to face her. Her nose almost touched mine.

I didn't step back this time. "Nobody treats my family this way. I've been thinking about leaving for days anyway, ever since Dr. Franklin told us about General Johnston coming."

"Is that so?"

I couldn't think of anything else polite to say, and I knew Ma wouldn't want me to say anything mean, no matter how awful Mrs. Franklin was. "Stay calm," Ma always preached. "There's no point screaming and yelling and carrying on. It doesn't do anybody any good."

"What are you thinking, Anna Green?" Mrs. Franklin asked.

I turned my head. Her breath was so bad. How could it smell like onions when we hadn't had any in weeks?

"Just what I thought. You ought to apologize right now. And I'll let you stay."

I looked her straight in the eyes. "No," I whispered.

Dr. Franklin came up behind his wife and took her arm. "Now, Mildred, let's just settle down. These children don't need to go anywhere tonight."

"Yes, we do, sir." I looked at him. "My ma would be disappointed if I stayed here any longer. We appreciate everything you've done to help us." I took a deep breath to gather more strength. "We need to do it on our own now."

"Thank goodness your ma isn't here to see how ungrateful you are." Mrs. Franklin struggled away from her husband.

"That's enough, Mildred." Dr. Franklin grabbed a hold of her arm again.

She whipped around faster than a dog chasing its tail. A whole minute passed before she said, "Yes, dear," in the quietest voice I'd ever heard her use. Then she jerked her arm free of his grasp and walked slowly, with her head held high, into her room. I held my breath, waiting for her to throw things at me. But she was silent.

Dr. Franklin put out his hand, like he wanted me to shake it. So, I did.

He clasped my hand between his. "You're doing the right thing. I know you can do this, now that you're ready."

"Sir—"

He held up his hand to stop me. "I'm sorry it had to come to this before you felt you could go back home."

Tears tried to pour out of my eyes, but I choked them back. He reminded me so much of Pa, and I ached to see Pa's face and hear his voice telling me the things Dr. Franklin had just said. When he let go of my hand, he walked slowly into the room with his wife.

"Anna, I'll help carry your things," Albert said.

I wanted to throw myself into his arms and have him tell me everything would be fine. But instead I said, "Thank you. That would be nice."

"Don't get involved in this, Albert," Mrs. Whitcock said, still rocking in her chair. Penelope and Nellie stood behind her.

"Mother, I have to help," he said.

She pushed her needle into the material and sighed. "You are your father's boy."

Then Penelope untied her ribbons from the ends of her braids and handed them to Sara. My sister looked at me to see if she could keep them.

"Thank you, Penelope." I nodded at Sara before going into our room to pack.

I hurried to gather our few belongings. I hated these caves in spite of their protection. The stuffiness struck me like a sickness while mosquitoes bit my arms and neck. Even with candles lit, the dark seemed worse inside than outside. What would we use for light in our cave if the candles were gone? There was no fuel left anywhere for lanterns. I closed our trunk as I tried to close my mind on these worries.

Albert and James picked up the chest, one at each end. Tying Sara's bonnet, I thought of Ma telling us to always cover our heads to keep from catching cold. I grabbed my sister's hand, and we followed Albert and James past Mrs. Franklin, who was back in her rocker and sewing again.

"Take care, children," Dr. Franklin said. "I'll check on you soon." He packed a pipe at the table. It was the first time I'd ever seen him with one and figured Mrs. Franklin had driven him to take up smoking. Across from him, Stuart watched his every move.

"Thank you, sir," I said and added, "for everything."

We rushed into the night with my knees shaking. When we passed Olivia still working in the yard, she whispered to me, "Good for you, Miss Anna. I knew you was brave."

Olivia. I felt awful for leaving her behind. "Take care. I'm not going to forget you," I told her. I needed to figure out a way to get her from Mrs. Franklin, but that would have to wait. Right now, I had to concentrate on getting James and Sara back to our home safely. It wouldn't do anybody any good if I tried to do too much.

I felt as small as a mouse scurrying through a cornfield, trying to find its way. But even a mouse gathers food for its family and makes a place for them to live in spite of the owls in the sky or the mousetraps on the ground. I certainly was as brave as a mouse. Starting small never hurt anybody.

— CHAPTER 23 —
Missing Ma

Although it was too dark to see my hand in front of my face, James and Albert practically ran with our trunk. I dragged Sara along to keep up with them. We were all afraid someone might jump out and rob us. Why did we leave at night? What if our cave was gone? What if the Yankees had done something awful to George and Noah?

Ma, I'm not sure if I'm making the right choice. Is this what you would have done? You stayed strong when Nellie died, and our men left. You only let us worry about the war when it put us in danger. I want to do the same for Sara and James. I think I can—NO, there's no thinking about it. I have to do this for them, for Michael, for you, and Pa. I know I can. I have to stop doubting myself, or we'll never make it.

In spite of my fears, we made the trip across town without any trouble. When we reached our house, we dashed past it to the cave where light came out. I prayed it was the servants in there and not a stranger or even worse, a Yankee.

Before I could tell James to wait, he went on in and yelled, "George, it's us!"

"Mr. James," George said. "You best be gettin' back before Missus Franklin notice. Mr. Albert, what are you doing with that trunk?"

Stepping into the light, I smiled at George and Noah. When they saw me, they both stood. "Why heaven's sakes, Miss Anna and Miss Sara, too."

"We've come home," I cried. Then the whole story spilled out of me like a steam engine barreling down its tracks.

"Mr. Michael is alive?"

"That's right." James opened the trunk and rummaged through it.

"Hallelujah!" George clapped his hands. Then he patted Noah on the shoulder. They both walked toward the back exit.

"Where're you going?" Sara held on tight to Betty.

"Miss Sara, we is gonna stay right out here and watch out for yous," George answered, then turned toward me. "We ain't got much to eat in the mornin', but there's some."

"Thank you, George," I said. "It's just nice to be home."

While Albert watched me, I unpacked our trunk, first removing the quilt. I tried to think of something to say, to thank him for his help. Everything I thought of seemed silly.

James broke the silence. "Albert, let's finish playing checkers."

"Nah, I can't." He put his hands in his pockets. "I've got to get back."

"You're just scared I'd beat you, and you'd know I was smarter," James said.

I started to scold my brother, but Albert was grinning. They reminded me of James and Michael teasing each other, and my chest started to ache. It always did when I thought of our family and the way things used to be.

"I'll be able to come by some, Anna." Albert walked into the night, and I followed him.

"Thank you."

He reached for my hand, and it looked like he wanted to say something. He opened his mouth a couple of times, but nothing came out. The bees inside my stomach were really buzzing, and I hoped my hand wasn't shaking as hard as I thought it was.

"Albert, are you all right?"

"Yes, it's just—"

"What?"

"I'm just glad you stood up to my aunt tonight. You'll be fine here. You've got some good slaves, and you're a smart girl. Besides, all this will be over soon."

I closed my eyes and prayed for God to put some words in my mouth that I could say back to this boy, but he didn't. I was left to my own ideas, so I said, "Sure." That was it. That was all I could think to say.

He smiled, and I managed to smile back. Then he did the most surprising thing. He leaned down and kissed my hand before he turned and left. I stood there watching him with a weird feeling that went all the way to my toes. And I wished more than ever I had my ma. She would know what to do and what he meant when he kissed my hand and why I could never think of anything to say when I was usually good with words.

After he left, I had more energy than a coon dog on a hunt, so I busied myself making a place for us to sleep. I was home! While hurrying through the cave, unpacking our trunk and lighting only two candles, our house caught my eye. I stood at the cave's entrance to see if I could find any damage, trying not to see the spot where Ma had lain, trying to think of anything but that day.

James helped distract me with his usual chatter. "Thank you for bringing us home."

I nodded at him, not used to his thanking anybody for anything.

He stood at the entrance with me. "Remember that one Easter, when we all tried to make breakfast for Ma and Pa? You know Nellie had gone to a slave service, and Michael said it would be easy."

"And you dropped the whole skillet of eggs and ham on the floor?"

He grinned. "I guess I wasn't as strong as I thought back then."

"I don't remember that," Sara said.

"You were only three." I picked her up and twirled her around, then pictured us in the kitchen and tried to get lost in those memories. But being back here brought the ache for Ma and Pa right to the center of my heart.

Yes, I was home. I had done the right thing, but sadness filled me. I thought I'd finally feel better, just being here. But something was still missing—would it always feel this way?

When I finished tidying up the cave, we lay down on a mattress with our quilt spread on it, and Sara and James soon were breathing heavy. Every time I closed my eyes, I saw Ma lying and bleeding in the grass.

Thunder rolled through the sky, and Sara snuggled closer. I worried muddy water might stream into our cave if it rained all night. But the storm also meant drinking water, and I knew we were short on that.

I got up to check on the weather. Looking out, I saw lightning flash across the dark sky. The rain slowed to a gentle pitter-patter. George and Noah were collecting pans full of rainwater, bringing them under the back porch of our house, and putting out empty pots. We sure were lucky to have them and lucky they didn't join up with the Yankees.

I wished I could have brought Olivia with me tonight. She needed to get away from Mrs. Franklin. I won't let Olivia stay there too much longer. I had to think of something.

We should have come back to our cave before now, but I wasn't ready to face the memories. I had to start being brave for my family. I felt sorry for making James live with that awful woman and for separating us from Sara. I would make it up to them as soon as Grant stopped shooting at us day and night.

I thought about Mrs. Franklin and what James told me about her giving food to a couple of Yankee soldiers. And what about that one morning when I heard her talking to someone outside the cave? Who was that? A plan formed in my mind—maybe there was a way to persuade Mrs. Franklin to give us Olivia.

In the morning, I woke after sleeping only a few hours and lit a candle to check for any damage in the cave. A small puddle lay in one corner with drops from the roof still plopping into it. I got a cloth and wiped it up while bombs screeched overhead. One hit the ground near us, shaking James and Sara awake.

"I'm starving." My brother complained as he walked outside the cave.

"James, get back in here," I said.

He looked up at the sky like I hadn't said anything.

"When do we get to see Michael?" Sara asked.

I knew she would want to see him, but I didn't think she should go to the hospital. That place could give her awful nightmares. "Michael can't have too many visitors until his bandage comes off."

"Oh." She stared at her feet.

My heart sank as I watched her sad face. "But you could give me something to take to Michael, to let him know you're thinking about him."

"I want to give it to him myself."

I gathered her in my arms. "Do you want Michael to come home soon?"

"Yes."

"Then he needs to get as much rest as he can. But I bet he'd like to have Betty visit and stay with him while he's in bed."

She smiled and handed me her doll.

James came inside and stood in front of me. "I'm going with you, and Sara can't stay here by herself."

"You're not going," I said.

"I am going. You're not in charge of me." James picked a rock off the floor and threw it in the air.

"Yes, I am in charge of you, of both of you. I'm the oldest. You are going to listen to me." I looked at James, and he had tears rolling down his face. I hadn't seen him cry much—even through all these terrible things that had happened to us.

"I just want to see Michael," he said.

I understood what he meant, and I'd probably feel the same way if I hadn't seen him already. "All right," I said. "We'll all go for a bit when the cannons stop."

George and Noah brought us breakfast from a nearby cave where they were staying with other slaves. Along with a cup of water, we each got a piece of pea bread and a slice of bacon. While we ate, shells exploded around the cave. Sara put a finger in each ear and squeezed her eyes shut. Our plates rattled on the table, and we coughed from the dust stirring up in the air.

James finished his bacon in two bites. "I'm still hungry."

I thought of the way his pants hung off him, too loose around the waist. They had fit perfectly at the beginning of the summer. "Here, take mine." I handed him the half piece I had left.

He gobbled it up and mumbled, "Thanks."

I prayed the shelling would stop soon, so we could be together with Michael. How long would we be able to endure this?

— CHAPTER 24 —

A Quiet Time

After waiting all morning for the bombing to stop, when we arrived at the Balfour house, Michael was sleeping. My heart sank into my stomach when I saw him. I hoped he'd be awake and waiting for me to visit again, but he needed his rest. We'd just have to wait for him.

The room smelled worse than I remembered, and Sara coughed so hard, tears fell from her eyes. We bumped into the cots and even soldiers' feet as we tried to walk through the room. More wounded had come in that morning. The flies buzzed more, and it felt hotter than ever.

Sara stayed right by my side, clutching my hand with her sweaty one. I knew she shouldn't have come here and imagined she would be right back to screaming in her sleep and wanting my arms around her like a few weeks ago.

James headed straight for Michael. We followed him, and I grabbed his arm before he could reach the cot.

"What do you think you're doing?" I asked.

"I'm waking Michael up. I want to talk to him." James tried to jerk away, but I held on tight.

"He needs to rest. I want him to come home." I pushed James over to the corner. Even if Michael came home now, I knew it wouldn't be the way I had hoped a while back. He would not be able to come home and take care of everything for James, Sara, and me. I would be taking care of him instead. But after all I'd been through this summer, I would be fine.

While we waited for Michael to wake, I looked for Molly but didn't see her. Doctors and nurses hurried about, helping the soldiers who shrieked and groaned in pain. Sara cried harder and harder. My first day in charge of this family, and I had already made a mistake. I pulled her real close and whispered, "Just close your eyes and think about the time when Michael made the swing for you. Remember? You played on it all day. You even learned how to push yourself by the end of the day—sticking your feet out, pulling them in, sticking them out, pulling them in." Pretty soon, she stopped crying, and her feet started moving like she was back on that swing.

James stood as still as a tree's branches on a hot, windless day, like he finally realized where we were and how awful it was. I wanted to tell him, "I told you so," but held my tongue.

While Sara kept her eyes closed, James and I watched a boy take his last breath with his pa kneeling right beside him. The man cried, "My boy!" and pounded his fists on the floor. Shutting my eyes, I remembered James hitting his fists on the ground the day Ma died. I said a quick prayer that we wouldn't hear our own pa cry out for Michael. He would be just fine, once he got that bandage off and was able to sit or walk by himself and come home.

Michael finally woke, and he struggled to sit. We rushed over to his cot, and Sara jumped onto his lap, clutching him tight. Even James hugged him. For a few moments, it seemed like we were the only people in the room.

On the next cot, Hank played *Bonnie Blue Flag* on his harmonica—the same song Ma used to sing. And we all shouted, "Hurrah! Hurrah!" during the chorus, like we had the day the shells flew over us while we baked bread and played dominoes.

"Children, be quiet," scolded a stocky nurse with her arms full of bandages. "There are sick men in here. This is not a celebration."

"Seems to me the place needs a little cheerin' up," Hank said. "A tune does that right fine."

The nurse leaned over him. "Sir, I'll have to re-move your instrument."

"I'd just like to see you try." He placed it under-neath his behind. I had to cover my mouth to keep from laughing.

"We understand, ma'am," Michael said. "I'm happy to see my family, that's all."

She wrinkled her nose and hurried off to help a man asking for a drink.

"Sara, I think you've grown taller than the shed behind our house." Michael took a deep breath, and I could tell he was putting up a good front for Sara and James. He was exhausted—his face pale with dark circles under his eyes.

"You don't make any sense," James said. "If she's that tall, than I must be taller than the courthouse."

"That's what I was just about to say." Michael laughed, but then he coughed and coughed. I grabbed a canteen of water, sitting on the stool between Hank and him, and gave my brother a drink.

Two men dressed in gray uniforms with gold buttons and several medals stood between the rows of cots, close to the end of Michael's bed.

"Good morning," the shorter man said. He took off his hat and held it over his heart. "We're just coming by to check on y'all."

"That's mighty nice," Hank said as he and Michael saluted.

"How're you doing, son?" The taller one, with more medals, which probably meant he was a colonel or somebody high up, asked Michael.

"I'm just fine, sir. Still got my legs and arms, still able to fight one day."

The colonel smiled at Michael and looked real proud of him. I couldn't believe my brother still wanted to fight in the war, after his injuries and knowing a shell had killed Ma. Maybe he wasn't thinking straight since he had that bandage around his head too tight.

"Any word about Johnston?" Hank asked, breaking the silence.

The shorter man sat down on the end of Hank's bed. "General Johnston is supposed to be on his way with more than enough troops to defeat the Feds. We just need to hold out a few more days."

On his harmonica, Hank played again, "Hurrah! Hurrah! For Southern Rights! Hurrah!"

The colonel patted his fellow soldier on the back and looked directly at Michael. "There's been no official word from Johnston," he said. "I don't believe he's coming."

"Johnston's not coming?" I placed my hand over my mouth as soon as the words popped out. Speaking out like that to a colonel was something James would do. But Johnston had to come! Everyone was waiting for him. Albert thought our lives would be back to normal when he came.

The colonel shook his head. "Our men are starving. We're running out of supplies. We'll be out of water soon."

Hank dropped his harmonica and opened his mouth to speak, but Michael beat him to it. "Are you talking about surrendering, sir?"

"If we surrender, we'll become prisoners of the Yankees. Please don't allow that, sir," I said.

"Surrender?" James's mouth opened wide. "The Yankees can't take us over!" He shook his hands with each word.

Michael took hold of James's arm and put his finger to his lips telling him to quiet down.

"Ah, General Pemberton is a good negotiator," the colonel said. "He won't let that happen." He placed his hand on the other man's shoulder. "Come, we need to look for our men among the wounded." Then he shook Michael's and Hank's hands and went on.

"Prisoners?" James yelled. "You and Hank will be prisoners?" He wiped his eyes with the back of his hand.

"No, James," Michael said, "You heard the colonel. They won't let that happen."

"That's right, young man." Hank patted his cot and scooted over for James to take a seat. "Grant wants this city 'cause it's on the river—he don't give a care about a bunch of worn-out troops."

"Maybe they'll let you go home," I said, hoping Hank was right. Why would Grant want our soldiers? Seemed like he had plenty already.

"Goin' home sure would be nice." Hank played his harmonica softly.

"It sure would," I said.

Michael wrapped his arms around Sara and winked at me. "It sure would, Squash."

We spent the next couple of hours talking about old times. Michael told the story of when James was born in the middle of the night, and Pa ran over to the neighbor's house to ask them to get Dr. Franklin. The only problem was he had forgotten to put his pants on, and his long johns were loose around his waist. They were falling down while he started the fire to boil some water. Finally Michael realized and said, "Pa, you forgot your pants!"

We all laughed before getting quiet and wondering if Pa was safe and if he would ever return to Vicksburg.

During the noon meal, we decided to head back to our cave. Michael fell asleep as soon as he finished eating his food. He seemed so tired, but that was probably normal with the injuries he had.

Sara's face was beet red, and I worried she would never recover from this visit. Many people seemed to be getting sick these days, probably because nobody was eating enough food. Sara was so skinny the summer breeze could have blown her over. I would need to give her my share of meat this evening. The last thing I wanted to happen was for her to become ill, also.

Sara didn't want to go to the hospital again. She said the place stunk too bad and had scary men in it. She didn't understand why Michael couldn't just come home. I asked the Lohrses if she could stay with them whenever we went to visit. And they agreed, especially because Emily missed Sara so badly.

For the next few days, we got up with the sun, ate a tiny breakfast in our cave until the bombs stopped, and then James and I took Sara to the Lohrses before making our way to the hospital, usually staying until supper. We fetched water, passed out food, and sat with men who needed to tell someone their stories. James surprised me at how well he got along with the soldiers. For once, it seemed like he was thinking about somebody besides himself. Michael grew stronger each day, but he still got tired and had trouble sitting up in bed for very long.

When we walked home one night, the whole city seemed too quiet. There wasn't any shooting on the battlefield. People came out of their caves and paced back and forth, like they didn't know what to do without bombs flying over their heads. Nobody talked much.

I thought when the noise stopped, we'd have a big celebration. But folks reminded me more of going to a funeral instead of a social.

"What's going on?" James looked around at the neighbors.

"I don't know," I said. "Let's ask Reverend Lohrs."

When we got to the Lohrses' house, they were watching Emily and Sara run and leap over craters in the backyard. The girls chased each other, giggling and falling to the ground when one caught the other. "Good evening." Reverend Lohrs removed his hat. "It's awful quiet tonight."

"Yes, sir," I answered. "What's it all about?"

Mrs. Lohrs patted her brow with a handkerchief. "There's talk of surrender, dear."

"No!" James cried and stomped the ground.

"Son, people are starving, and we're short on water. No rain for days." Reverend Lohrs placed his arm around James. "We'll be fine whatever happens."

James broke away from him. "We're not cowards."

"No, but we're humans, and we can only stand so much," Mrs. Lohrs said. "Mrs. Gordon told me the other day they had to kill their canary for soup meat. Their boy was sick, and they needed something to give him strength. They had nothing else to feed him."

I knew she was right, and we were always hungry. If the siege went on much longer, we'd be starving soon. James and Sara didn't know, but George had to feed us a rat the last couple of days. I ate the meat, although it was awfully hard to swallow down just thinking about how rats ran through the streets and got into awful things. But I had to pretend it was rabbit so my brother and sister would eat. In spite of that, I still didn't want to give in to the Yanks. I'd eat twenty rats if I had to.

If we surrendered, Grant could demand anything; and since we were desperate, we might accept it. What if he took our soldiers as prisoners, even the wounded ones? I might never see Michael again. We were finally getting back together. I couldn't stand to be separated now.

The next morning, James stayed in bed, feeling ill. I touched his forehead to see if he had a fever, and it felt hot like he'd been in the sun all day. George went to fetch Dr. Franklin while I wiped James's brow. Sara sang songs quietly, but she only knew the words to a few, so she just kept singing the same ones over and over. Obviously, James was sick because he never said a word about it.

While I sat by James's bed and held a cloth on his head, I tried not to think of what Molly had said about Baby Peter. She told us yesterday that her son wasn't eating his food and was very weak. She didn't say it, but I could tell by the sound of her voice that there wasn't much hope for her baby, especially with so many of our supplies blocked by the Yanks. I hoped James didn't have the same illness as Baby Peter.

"Come on, James." I brushed his hair back from his eyes. "Wake up. Don't you hear Sara singing?"

His eyes fluttered and then closed again. It was going to be up to Sara and me to take care of this family for a while. My brothers were usually strong—they had strength in their blood. I hoped more than anything they would get better.

The cannons remained quiet, and I figured we'd hear news of surrendering soon. The silence made my head hurt almost worse than the shells. Thoughts of life with the Yankees in control whirled through my mind like a swing wound up tight and let go. I knew I was going loony because I wanted to hear the shelling again. Then it meant we were still fighting, and Michael wouldn't become a prisoner. But what about James and Baby Peter? They needed medicine, and if the siege was over, we might have supplies soon.

A loud steam whistle from the river interrupted my thoughts.

"What's that?" Sara jumped from her stool.

"I don't know." I went outside to check.

Our neighbors were all outside their caves, too. Some were looking toward the waterfront; some were looking up the road. The Yankee ships on the Mississippi, decorated with red, white, and blue banners, blew their whistles like they were having a celebration.

That could only mean one thing. The siege was over. A ribbon of blue men marched from the battlefield. Folks hugged each other tight, and I heard a baby scream.

A Yankee soldier rode past on his horse, shouting, "Vicksburg's surrendered! Grant makes his way to the courthouse."

I pinched myself on the arm, hoping this was a nightmare. "Ow!" I rubbed the spot and knew it was real—we had lost.

— CHAPTER 25 —
Surrender!

Fred Pearson, a boy James's age, threw pebbles at the Yankee soldier as he galloped away. More Blue Bellies, hundreds of them, carried a worn-out Union flag and marched behind the soldier on the horse. Our women cried, and the men yelled curse words and spat at the troops' feet when they passed. Mrs. Pearson, Fred's ma, fell on her knees and wept while her husband removed his hat and placed it over his heart. I didn't care about much right now, except finding out what would happen to Michael and seeing if the Yankees would give us some medicine and food.

Our neighbors followed the army on their way to the courthouse, and Sara and I went, too, leaving James with Dr. Franklin. I just kept praying James was going to be well. Everybody was ill now and then and recovered just fine.

My stomach did somersaults on our walk to the courthouse, and I clutched Sara's hand tight. She kept trying to get loose, but I wasn't going to take a chance of losing her in this crowd.

"Where are we going?" she asked. "What are we doing?"

I didn't answer—she'd find out soon enough.

Once we reached the courthouse, the Yankees rang the bell, and their band played happy tunes. The Yanks cheered when they lowered our flag and replaced it with theirs. They whooped it up on one side of the lawn, and our troops buried their faces in their hands on the other. Our men should have held their heads up. I wanted to thank every one of them for trying to save our city.

Sara stood next to me with tears streaming down her cheeks. "What's happening, Anna?"

"We lost," I told her. Did this mean Ma died for no reason? Our soldiers tried to fight the Yanks off, but maybe we should have given up right away. Then Ma would be alive, and Michael wouldn't be lying in a hospital bed. Maybe the whole South should give in to the Yankees—let President Lincoln be our leader again. Then Pa could come home, too. Would it really be so bad if we didn't have slaves anymore? At least families would be together, and people would be healthy.

I felt horrible thinking this way. My pa and brother wouldn't have left us in the first place if they didn't think this war was important. But honestly, part of me was happy that we wouldn't spend another night in a cave.

After the band stopped playing and some of our neighbors made their way back to their homes, Sara and I left. When we returned, we found George had moved James from the cave into the house and put him in our bed. I wondered if that was a good idea with the house being such a mess—dust, dirt, and black powder seemed to cover everything. But the cave was dark and damp and stuffy, which was no better.

Dr. Franklin checked over James while Sara and I waited in the corner. Beads of sweat shone on James's forehead, which hopefully meant his fever was breaking.

When Dr. Franklin finished, James said to us, "Where'd you go?" he whispered. His face was as white as the sheet he lay on, but his eyes were finally open.

I decided to lie. "Sara and I picked up shrapnel in the yard. Don't worry. We saved some for you for when you're feeling better." I didn't want him to know about the Yankees' flag on the courthouse. He'd get too upset and want to see it himself when he needed to stay in bed.

Dr. Franklin closed his leather bag. "Anna, wipe his brow and keep a wet cloth on his head. I've no medicine to give him, yet. I'll have to get some from the hospital if they've any to spare. He needs to eat and drink plenty, which may be hard to do."

"I'll give him my share," I said.

"You're a brave girl." Dr. Franklin placed his hand on my shoulder. "I'll come back at nightfall, hopefully with some tonic."

I followed Dr. Franklin to the front porch. "Have you heard news of the surrender? Will the Yankees give us supplies? What's Grant going to do with our soldiers?"

"Whoa—one question at a time." He smiled and scratched his head. "I'm not sure about the supplies. I hope we get something soon." He took a deep breath.

"As for the soldiers, I think he's going to let them come home. They'll have to promise not to bear arms against the North again."

A smile as big as Pa's prize-winning watermelons crossed my face. "You mean Michael might get to come home to recover completely?"

"I believe so." Dr. Franklin stepped off the porch. "Good day, Anna."

As I watched him walk away, there was another thing I needed to take care of soon. Since the night we'd returned to our cave, I had been thinking about my plan to help Olivia. Now with James sick, our house being such a mess, and Michael maybe coming home, it would sure be nice to have another pair of hands around here, and I thought she'd be happy to get away from the busybody. I hurried after the doctor and blurted, "Sir, I need a word with Mrs. Franklin."

He stopped and turned around with his mouth open. I was sure he didn't expect me to want to talk to her.

"I'm wondering if she'll be home today?"

He wiped his face with a handkerchief. "Yes, she's there now with Stuart. Albert and his ma and sisters went back to a new cave their servants built for them."

Albert. He hadn't visited in a couple of days, and that was probably why. "Thank you, sir. I'll call on your wife this afternoon, then."

I watched Dr. Franklin leave, thinking about what I would say to Mrs. Franklin. I wanted to ask her about giving food to the Yankees. I still had no real proof, but if I asked the right questions, she might wind up telling me. That's what Ma and Pa used to do to my siblings and me when we did something wrong. We always wound up telling on ourselves.

If I found out Mrs. Franklin was a traitor, she wouldn't want me to tell anyone. Maybe I could persuade her to give me Olivia, whom she didn't like much anyway. If that didn't work, I had a second plan with my jar of coins and an idea to pretend Stuart stole some money from us. The only thing I knew for certain was Mrs. Franklin cared about two things more than anything else. First her reputation and second her family. I would have to use one of those if I had any chance to save Olivia from her awful life.

I went back inside to check on James. He was sleeping, somewhat peacefully, with Sara still singing lullabies. I figured this would be a good time to go see Mrs. Franklin.

I found George cleaning in the kitchen. "George, I need to run an errand. Can you keep an eye on James and Sara for me? I'll be at the Franklins' for a while if anything happens."

He raised his eyebrows at me, also. Everyone seemed to know something was up. "Yes, Miss Anna."

I tied my bonnet and went to get Olivia.

— CHAPTER 26 —
A Turn of Events

I could hear Mrs. Franklin yelling at Olivia when I was standing on the road in front of their house. They were in the back, but her voice rang out like the cannons' blasts. "I said I needed the red dress for tonight, and it's still lying in a pile on my floor! Why can't you ever learn, girl?"

As I came around the house, Mrs. Franklin slapped Olivia across the face. "There'll be more of that if you can't learn your colors." She swished her skirt and headed toward the kitchen door.

A sick-nervous feeling crept through my body like a slow-dripping poison. I took a deep breath and called, "Mrs. Franklin. The doctor said I would find you here." The sun beat down on me, and I needed a drink of water badly. I didn't know how I was ever going to get the words out.

She let go of the door handle and turned around slowly. "Yes? What could you possibly want?"

I tried not to look at Olivia because I didn't want Mrs. Franklin to know that I cared anything about her

171

servant. I bit my lip and tried to remember what I had practiced on my way over.

"Some people are saying the Yankees will give us food and supplies now that their flag is hanging on our courthouse."

She looked at me and said nothing. My stomach grumbled from hunger as if even my body was trying to help Olivia.

I swallowed and twisted my braid. "We sure need the food, we—"

"Anna Green," she interrupted. "I hope you're not crawling back here, asking me for some food. You made your bed, now you must lie in it." She stared down her long, pointy nose.

"No, ma'am. I'm just wondering if you've been able to give food to anyone else. I know you can be quite generous, like you were with us when Ma passed." I swallowed hard, trying to keep my voice sounding sweet and not bitter.

"Why is that your concern?"

"I just thought I'd pass on the news to our neighbors about how generous you've been—that is if you've been giving food to anyone."

She turned toward the door. "I have an appointment I must prepare for. Good day."

She wasn't going to tell me anything. *Should I just come out and ask her if she gave food to the Yankees?* But I knew she'd never admit it. I didn't want her to go inside, so I started on my second plan. "I believe we left my mother's coin jar in your cave." I knew we hadn't. It was in my basket I had just sat on the ground. The jar kept rattling around in there, and I didn't want her to hear it. My heart beat faster. I knew I shouldn't lie, but it was the only way to beat Mrs. Franklin and have Olivia come live with us.

"No, I haven't seen it." She reached for the door handle again.

"Mrs. Franklin, we don't have it anymore. Do you think you could please check around and see if we left it in the cave?"

She stopped and swiveled her head.

"Or I could go look myself," I added. Then I could pretend like I found it in the cave and suggest maybe Stuart had hid it there. *God, please forgive me. I don't know what else to do.*

"I don't think so." She crossed her arms and turned her body to face me.

"Then, I guess I'll have to call on the sheriff and ask him to look into it."

She stared down her long, pointy nose. "Exactly what are you accusing me of, Anna Green?"

"I'm not accusing you of anything." I took a deep breath and kept fiddling with my braid. "The last place we had our coin jar was in your cave, and now we don't have it anymore. You haven't seen it, and you won't let me look around. So, I guess I'll have to let the sheriff know." I kicked at a rock buried in a small patch of grass. "Besides, you're probably just protecting Stuart, and I can't really blame you. I'd do the same thing for James."

"Listen here, young lady." Mrs. Franklin placed her hands on her hips like she always did when she got angry. "Stuart hasn't got your money. You probably need to look right in your own house—at your sneaky, thievin' brother."

"May I talk with Stuart?"

"No."

"Why not?"

This time, she got real close to my face, and I could smell her onion breath. "Because I'm telling you no. Now get off my property."

I still had no idea how I would convince her that she needed to give me Olivia. *God, please help me. I'm at a loss here.*

I smiled as sweetly as I could. "Mrs. Franklin, I'm sorry. I'll go home and ask James about it before I do anything else." I was stalling for time to come up with a third plan. What would Pa do?

"Then be on your way." Mrs. Franklin took her lacy handkerchief from her sleeve and blew her nose, sounding like a honking goose.

"My goodness, ma'am. Are you feeling sick?"

"Not until you showed up."

I bit my lip to keep from smarting off. "So many people seem to be getting sick. Your husband had to come see James today. He has a fever. How is Baby Peter?"

"That's none of your business!" She glared at me, worse than she did the night we left her cave. "I suggest you get out of here immediately, before I'm the one calling on the sheriff."

"But—"

She pointed her finger, reached for the doorknob, and left me there with tears in my eyes. The sick-nervous feeling was back and worse than ever. I had to help Olivia. She had helped me so much when I was with the Franklins, and now she was being punished because she didn't clean the right color dress? Mrs. Franklin probably told her the wrong one on purpose. And what was going on with Baby Peter?

I walked away toward the side of the house, picking up my basket along the way but not looking at Olivia.

At that moment, Stuart came running around from the front of the house and smacked into me. He knocked me and my basket down, and I knocked a note out of his hand.

"You stupid girl," he said. "You made me get my pants dirty."

I snatched up the note.

"Give me that," he said.

"Give me back my money jar." I stood and held the note above my head; and for the first time, I was thankful I was taller than a boy.

He stood, too. "I don't have your jar. What're you talking about?"

Stall, Anna, stall. "Well, we can't find it at home, and the last place we had it was here. That's what I was just telling your ma. She thinks you probably took it."

"You're a loon. Those bombs must have hit more than your ma."

I didn't even think about it. My fist just curled up on its own, swung from my hip, and punched Stuart right in the nose. He flew back to the ground and started screaming.

His screams brought Mrs. Franklin running from the house. If there was one thing you could say about the old busybody, it was that she loved her children.

"Anna Green!" she screamed. "What have you done now?"

Through blood and tears, Stuart answered for me. "She hit me."

"I told you to leave." Mrs. Franklin snatched her lacy handkerchief from her sleeve and held it on Stuart's nose. While she took care of him, I read the note. When I finished, I knew God was helping me, or maybe He was just trying to save Olivia.

I read out loud while Mrs. Franklin held the cloth to her son's nose. "Dear Aunt Mildred," I paused and looked her straight in the eye.

"Where'd you find that?" She was on her knees, no longer holding the cloth to Stuart's bleeding nose.

"Ma!"

"Hush-up, Stuart."

I continued reading, "I received your request for food and medicine. And although I know you helped me and my fellow Union soldiers when we were hungry throughout the siege, I'm not sure if I can give you special treatment now. If my captain were to find out, I would not be treated well. Southern sympathizers are not liked much in our army, as I'm sure you can understand. I will send Mother your best. She does like her home in Illinois. You should think about moving your family there and away from the traitors. All the best to you and yours. Your nephew, Benjamin."

Mrs. Franklin put her head in her hands and cried. That wasn't the reaction I expected. I thought she'd be angrier than ever before—angry with me, angry with this Benjamin person, and angry with Stuart for letting me see the note.

Stuart sat up—his nose had stopped bleeding. "I tried to hide it from you, Ma." He put his hand over hers. "Anna took it from me."

She patted his hand and continued to cry. I didn't know what to do. Should I apologize to her for reading the letter? No, she had been giving the Yankees food when the rest of us were starving. But it was her nephew, and she did love her family. Now, he wasn't showing her any loyalty at all. But why should she get extra food when the rest of us would probably get slop from the Yankees, if anything? She didn't have any right to ask him for special treatment. But wouldn't I do the same thing for James and Sara if I knew a Blue Belly? Yes. I kneeled down next to her.

"What do you want?" She wiped her tears on her sleeve since her handkerchief was stained red.

I started to place my hand on hers and Stuart's, but then stopped. Instead, I folded my hands in prayer and said, "Dear God, please help the Franklins because they helped my family when we needed it. Bless us all and be with us during this uncertain time. And please help our servants. We don't mean to treat them so badly. Amen." I couldn't resist adding that last part.

Through shining tears, Mrs. Franklin said, "What do you want? Why won't you leave? Whatever you're planning to do, just do it. Tell everyone that I've been helping the Yankees. I don't care anymore. Baby Peter has been ill, and my own nephew, my oldest sister's boy, can't find it in his heart to help us. It just doesn't matter."

Should I just get up and leave her alone? I knew how awful she was feeling. I didn't want to feel sorry for this mean, nasty woman, but it was horrible to have

someone die that you loved so much. Mrs. Franklin
was worried about Baby Peter dying. It was a pain that
took forever to go away. I felt my pain every day when
I thought about Ma. Whoever thought Mrs. Franklin
and I would have anything in common? But I came here
for one reason, and I couldn't stop now. I needed to
gather the newest member of my family, Olivia, who
would help Sara and me while our men were sick,
wounded, and gone.

"I want Olivia."

"What?"

"I want Olivia. I'll give you the money we have saved,
and I won't tell anyone about your nephew."

"No way," Stuart said. "You're a loon."

Mrs. Franklin was quiet. Then she rose, went to
my basket and opened it, and took out the money jar.
"It's done." She turned and went into the house.

"Ma!" Stuart called. "My nose. Help me." He ran
after her.

I wasn't as sneaky as I thought with hiding the jar
in my basket, but at least I had Olivia now. She must
have heard the whole conversation because I found
her in the servants' quarters, packing a knapsack.

"Olivia," I said quietly. "I'm sorry I had to buy you.
We won't treat you badly."

She smiled at me, then looked up to Heaven.
"Thank you, Jesus." She tied her knapsack, and we
walked out of her quarters toward our new life.

— CHAPTER 27 —
Finding My Place

When Olivia and I returned home, George moved James to Ma and Pa's room and set up a bed for Sara and me in there, too. He and Noah must have swept and polished the whole room while I was gone because it looked like we could eat off the floor. We gave Olivia our room until George could make a separate place for her in the servants' quarters. It would take a while since there wasn't much spare wood to go around.

Since James was awake, I told him about my visit to the Franklins. Hearing about what I did seemed to make him stronger. "I knew she was giving the Blue Bellies food. I knew it," he said. His head felt cooler to the touch, but I wiped his face with a cloth anyway. I wanted to do everything I could to make sure he had a quick recovery.

When he fell asleep, I went to our bedroom to sweep the floor. I was the woman of the house now, and I wanted to clean it and make it nice for my family. The servants were busy preparing a meal for us and fixing up the kitchen. At suppertime, I would go on a quick visit to see Michael and find out what he knew about the surrender.

After a while, I needed some fresh air. The day was too hot to get much relief. A warm breeze met me while I rested on the porch, praying James would get better soon. I wouldn't allow myself to think anything else, although my tapping feet weren't listening to my brain.

Yankees marched back and forth on the road. Some laughed and pointed at my neighbors, taunting, "You want some food? How about some nice, juicy rats?" Other soldiers handed out bread and fruit to the people on the street. I received a loaf of bread and a jug of milk for my family. I wasn't happy to be taking this from our enemy, but I wanted James to get better, and I didn't want Sara to starve and become ill.

I saw Mrs. Pearson chasing a couple of soldiers. She held her parasol in the air and shouted, "Y'all give me my silver back this instant, or I'll knock your heads into Louisiana." The men ran out of sight without dropping her silver. I wished for the first time in a long time that I had some paper and ink to write down what was happening.

I turned to go back inside to James but saw the Reverend coming down the road with a package in his hand.

"Good evening, Reverend Lohrs."

"Good evening, dear. I think I've got something here you might want to see."

I took the small bundle and looked at the writing. It was from Pa! I ripped open the paper to find a letter, a journal, a tiny doll, and six marbles. "Thank you, Reverend. How'd you get this?"

"The Feds allowed me to receive some mail after they inspected it. I guess being the Reverend has some benefits." He removed his hat. "I explained this was from your pa, and the kind officer let me bring it to you. I'll let you alone to read your letter." He put his hat back on and left.

The letter was short, but I was glad to have it.

To my beloved children,

I received your letter today and am writing to you filled with terrible sorrow. I miss your ma greatly as I know you do. I am sorry I cannot be there with you. You must be strong and work together like your ma and I have taught you. Find your strength in God's love when you feel like you cannot go on. Please know that my thoughts are always with you, and I wish I could wrap my arms around each of you and comfort you.

Is Michael in Vicksburg as you thought? Send word soon if you have found him. News is spreading about people starving and living in the caves you wrote about. I hope this is not true as it breaks my heart to hear my dear children are suffering in such a way.

Please enjoy my gifts. It is all I can give you right now. I want to return to you as soon as I can to make sure you are surviving. I will have to wait for word from the general. I love you, children. Always remember that.

Love,
Pa

I reread the letter until I memorized his sweet words. Then, I folded it and gathered the doll and marbles to take them to Sara and James. I wished Pa could come home, so we could all be together. But at least he was alive. If General Lee didn't allow him to travel to Vicksburg, we would be disappointed, but we would make it until Pa could get to us. The South needed strong soldiers, and Pa was surely one of the best. It was important for my family to be together, but I was learning that sometimes we had to make sacrifices to help other people.

I had so much to think about. I couldn't wait to write in my new journal Pa sent me. But first I'd have to visit Mrs. Lohrs for a lesson. Just another thing I needed to learn—how to make ink from berries.

— EPILOGUE —
A Journal Entry

July 14, 1863

It's been ten days since we surrendered. I learned how to make this ink from pokeberry juice. It's hard to write with, and I have to dip my pen a lot more. But at least I'm writing again.

Michael came home. He's still awful tired and forgets things, like where he put his coffee or the day of the week. He doesn't have to go back to the army. Grant let the soldiers come home if they promised not to fight again. I'm sure some men lied, but not Michael. He said he's staying with us, although I wonder if he'll feel the same when he is fully recovered.

James's fever broke after a couple of days, and he's back to being a pest, but not as bad as before. He does yell at the Yankee soldiers when they pass in front of our house. I scold him for calling attention to us and worry they'll pick on us because of James's big mouth. He has been helping with Michael, though. James reads books to him since Michael's eyes don't always focus too well.

I've learned there are two sorts of Yankees. The first kind are generous. They give us food and water. Their doctors help our wounded. The second kind aren't so nice.

I heard a story about General Grant and his kindness, although it was hard for me to believe. How could someone with an ounce of kindness do what he did to Vicksburg? But as Pa always says, "People are seldom all one way or another."

The story goes like this. A lady complained to Grant about his troops stealing from her. She said they had even dug up the body of her poor baby, who had died a day earlier. I heard the soldiers had seen freshly dug soil and didn't believe the woman had buried her baby there. They thought the woman hid her valuables in the hole. But they found out she had told the truth after they finished digging. When she told her story to Grant, he rode off to find those soldiers and discipline them.

Those men were the same kind that took Mrs. Pearson's silver. When I told George about her chasing after those soldiers, he placed the few pieces of silver and jewelry that Ma and Pa owned, plus some money, into a cloth. Then he dug a deep hole right next to our house—I think he shoveled all night. He rolled our rainwater barrel over the spot to hide it.

And the Yanks did come. They took a mirror, some dishes, and fruit another Yankee soldier had given me. They said our things were better than what they had. Each day, I worry about them coming back and stealing our food. We eat without hardly taking a breath.

George and Noah are fixing our roof above the kitchen now. They have to use wood from a neighbor's barn for lumber. Olivia does most of the cooking, and James is sure happy. She cooks as well as Nellie did, so we don't have to eat my hard biscuits. With Olivia's help, I'm using scraps of material from clothes that no longer fit us to make a quilt for the winter. Our supplies are still low, and I don't think things will ever be back to normal.

I miss Ma terribly. Sometimes when I start thinking about her, I try to stop because it makes me so sad. But the more I try to quit, the more her face stays with me. I see her smile at Sara, and then scold James or tell me to keep working on my bread because it'll turn out sooner or later. I think someday I'll write down each memory, so we don't forget. Then I can share them with my children and my brothers' and sister's, too. Ma will live forever in our hearts and minds.

I see Albert coming down the road, so that's all I'm writing today. He's come by a few times to check on us and make sure we've got enough to eat. I can't help but smile when I see his handsome face, and I wonder if that's the way Ma felt about Pa. I guess I'll have to write more about that tomorrow.

Educational Resources

— AUTHOR'S NOTE —

Although Anna Green is a fictional character, the Siege of Vicksburg was very real. Anna experiences the same difficulties and hardships as Vicksburg's citizens did during the six weeks the Yankees shot at them day and night.

Yes, people actually lived in "caves," which the slaves dug out of the yellow clay hills. This is how the citizens protected themselves from the Yankees' weapons. Families really did put furniture and personal belongings in the caves to make them more like home. Union soldiers called Vicksburg "Prairie Dog Village."

To us, living in the 21st century, it may seem difficult to believe that shells flew overhead, exploded in a house, and only damaged one room or even just a roof. The important fact to remember is these "bombs," as the citizens called them, were not as powerful as the kind you may have seen on television. As a matter of fact, if you ever go to Vicksburg, you can actually tour houses that still have unexploded cannonballs lodged in the wall. It is also true that the shelling seemed to stop three times a day, when the Yankee soldiers ate their meals.

Still, Vicksburg's citizens lived in danger every day, even in the caves. Caves did collapse some of the time and kill people. Diseases, such as diphtheria, which Baby Peter had, ran rampant through the city. There were very few supplies to treat these illnesses.

The biggest problem for the citizens, besides living in fear of a shell striking them, was the shortage of supplies. Food was the number one problem, and people used substitutes just like in the story. They ground peas to make bread, and it tasted awful. The bread was either rubbery or hard as a rock. When meat became scarce, rats, horses, and mules were used as meat instead of cattle and pigs. *The Daily Citizen* was actually printed on the back of wallpaper!

In spite of these hardships, the citizens of Vicksburg were proud of their city and did not want to surrender. Emma Balfour, who lived in the city during the siege, kept a diary that is in print today. (The Balfour house in Anna's story is based on the actual Balfour house, which is still standing.) In Mrs. Balfour's diary, she wrote about how the Yankees fired at the women and children in the caves because they thought General Pemberton, a Confederate leader, would surrender quickly. Mrs. Balfour emphasized the women and children had strong spirits, and this was evident when a petition was started. The petition basically stated that if enough signatures were obtained on the petition, the firing would stop, and the women and children could leave the city. According to Mrs. Balfour, only three people signed it, and that was not enough! So most people stayed in the city and lived in their caves.

However, General Pemberton did finally surrender on July 4, 1863. He thought if he surrendered on Independence Day, General Grant would give him better terms. General Grant did allow the Confederate soldiers, like Michael and Hank, to go home if they promised not to bear arms against the North. Yankee soldiers celebrated and marched to the courthouse to raise their flag. The people of Vicksburg were devastated, and the Fourth of July holiday was not celebrated in the city for more than eighty years after that day of surrender.

If you have more questions on what is fact and what is fiction about the Siege of Vicksburg, please see my Web site, www.margodill.com, where you can contact me with any questions!

If you want to read more about the Siege of Vicksburg, check out these books.

For kids:

The Tamarack Tree by Patricia Clapp. Lothrop, Lee and Shephard Books, 1986.

Ghosts of Vicksburg by Kathleen Ernst. White Mane Kids, 2003.

For teachers and parents:

My Cave Life in Vicksburg by A Lady (Mary Webster Loughborough). Reprinted by the Vicksburg and Warren County Historical Society, 1990.

Vicksburg: A City Under Siege (Diary of Emma Balfour, May 16, 1863–June 2, 1863).

Vicksburg: Fall of the Confederate Gibraltar by Terrence J. Winschel. McWhiney Foundation Press, 1999.

— DISCUSSION QUESTIONS —

For more lesson plan ideas and activities, please see www.margodill.com.

Part One

1. Why do you think Anna's ma tells her that family is the most important thing and to never forget that?
2. Why does General Grant want to take over Vicksburg?
3. Describe the Green family's cave.
4. Why do George and Noah stay outside the cave?
5. Why is it difficult to see if Michael is with the soldiers in chapters two and three?
6. In chapter four, Sara and Anna are worried because it is too quiet. What do they mean by this?
7. What are some of James's actions that show that he is "man of the house"? Do you think he is acting like a "man of the house"?
8. How does Reverend Lohrs help Anna and her siblings?

Part Two

1. What are some of the memories Anna has during Ma's funeral?

2. How does Mrs. Franklin's news of James and Anna coming to live with her affect Anna?

3. If you had a journal like Anna's, what would you write in it?

4. Why do you think Mrs. Lohrs didn't tell Anna and her siblings about their going to live with Mrs. Franklin? Do you think it's a good idea for Anna and James to go to the Franklins?

5. How does Mrs. Franklin treat the slaves that work for her? Compare and contrast Mrs. Franklin's behavior toward her slaves with Anna's family's behavior.

6. Why does Anna believe her pa and Michael joined the Confederate army? Do you agree or disagree with their reasons?

7. What are three substitutes that the Vicksburg citizens used because they did not have enough supplies?

8. Describe what it would be like to live in a cave based on descriptions in the story.

9. Why does Dr. Franklin believe people set fire to the stores downtown?

10. Do you think Anna should have thrown her journal in the fire or let Mrs. Franklin read it? Do you have another way to hide it from Mrs. Franklin? Explain your answer.

11. Whom do you agree with when it comes to signing the petition about leaving Vicksburg: Mrs. Franklin, who wants to sign it, or Dr. Franklin, who won't sign it? Why?

12. What are some emotions Anna is feeling when she discovers the letter is for Molly?

13. Describe the army hospital in your own words.

14. When Anna realizes she will have to tell Michael about Ma's death, she is scared and asks Molly to get her father. Molly tells her she will have to tell Michael herself. Do you agree with Molly? Do you think Anna is the one to tell Michael? Explain your answer.

15. Should Sara have stayed with the Lohrses until Anna and James could go back home, or was it a good idea she came to live with the Franklins? Explain your answer.

16. Why do you think Michael wants Anna to tell him a story?

Part Three

1. Why did Anna finally decide to take James and Sara home? Do you think it was the right decision? Explain why or why not.

2. What are some worries Anna has about going home?

3. When James, Sara, and Anna visit Michael in the hospital, they talk to two Confederate leaders. What does the one man reveal to the children?

4. Why is Anna scared of surrendering to the Yankees?

5. What are some of the ways the Yankees celebrate their victory?

6. How does Anna feel about the surrender?

7. What are the two ways Anna tries to get Mrs. Franklin to release Olivia?

8. How does Anna succeed in getting Olivia?

9. Why are the three gifts Pa sends perfect for his children?

10. Why isn't Anna as worried as she used to be when she hears Pa may not come home for a while? Do you think she has changed since the beginning of the story? How?

11. Describe Albert and how he is important to the story.

12. What are the two kinds of Yankees?

— THE AUTHOR —

 Margo L. Dill is an author, speaker, and freelance editor and writer. Her writings have appeared in various magazines, newsletters, anthologies, and websites. She holds a bachelor's degree in English and a master's degree in elementary education from Truman State University in Missouri. A member of the Society of Children's Book Writers and Illustrators, she resides in St. Louis with her family and dogs.

— OF RELATED INTEREST —

GHOSTS OF VICKSBURG
By Kathleen Ernst

Jamie Carswell, a young soldier with the 14th Wisconsin Infantry Regiment, is haunted by the civilian suffering he witnesses while campaigning in Mississippi. His favorite cousin, Althea, is already tormented by a past mistake when she finds herself trapped inside Vicksburg during the Union army's sieges in 1863. *Ghosts of Vicksburg* is the compelling story of two young people struggling to find their way during one of the most dramatic campaigns of the Civil War.

ISBN 978-1-57249-322-3 · Softcover

RETREAT FROM GETTYSBURG
By Kathleen Ernst

A Williamsport boy faces difficult choices when rising Potomac River floodwater traps the Confederate army trying to reach Virginia after its battle at Gettysburg. His patriotic feeling is tested when in caring for a wounded Confederate, he recognizes the humanity of the other side.

"An excellent example of how to teach history through fiction."
—*School Library Journal*

ISBN 978-1-57249-403-9 · Softcover

WHITE MANE PUBLISHING CO., INC.

To Request a Catalog Please Write to:
WHITE MANE PUBLISHING COMPANY, INC.
P.O. Box 708 • Shippensburg, PA 17257
e-mail: marketing@whitemane.com
Our Catalog is also available online
www.whitemane.com

CPSIA information can be obtained at www.ICGtesting.com
Printed in the USA
BVOW020139190912

300721BV00004B/1/P